THE PET FINDERS CLUB

THE PET FINDERS CLUB

THE PET FINDERS CLUB

Come Back, Buddy!

BEN M. BAGLIO

Hodder
Children's
Books

A division of Hachette Children's Books

Special thanks to Liss Norton

Text copyright © 2004 Working Partners Ltd
Illustration copyright © 2007 Cecilia Johansson

First published in the USA in 2004 by Scholastic Inc

First published in Great Britain in 2007
by Hodder Children's Books

The rights of Ben M Baglio and Cecilia Johansson to be
identified as the Author and Illustrator of the Work respectively
have been asserted by them in accordance with the
Copyright, Designs and Patents Act 1988

1

ISBN-10: 0 340 93130 2
ISBN-13: 978 0 340 93130 1

Typeset in Weiss by Avon DataSet Ltd,
Bidford on Avon, Warwickshire

Printed in the UK by CPI Bookmarque, Croydon, CR0 4TD

The paper and board used in this paperback by Hodder Children's
Books are natural recyclable products made from wood grown in
sustainable forests. The manufacturing processes conform to the
environmental regulations of the country of origin.

Hodder Children's Books
a division of Hachette Children's Books
338 Euston Road
Lonwon NW1 3BH

Chapter One

Andi Talbot was lost. Not just a little bit lost, as if she'd turned right instead of left at the last corner, but totally, utterly lost, without the tiniest clue about how to find her house again.

"Where on earth are we, Buddy?" she asked, bending down to stroke her Jack Russell terrier.

Buddy pricked up his ears and licked her hand, but for once, it didn't make Andi feel better. She gazed round, wondering if she could see anything that would let her know where she was. But this road was just like the others she had walked along so far, lined with tall, shady trees, their leaves just turning red and gold for autumn, so that it was impossible to see the houses behind them. Andi loved trees – especially if they were good to

1

climb – but these were no help at all in finding her way home!

Straightening up, she hurried along the street, searching for a landmark that would tell her she was heading in the right direction. A long line of distant green-grey mountain peaks stretched along the horizon, just showing above the roofs and treetops. Andi felt a tingle in her stomach as she looked at them – back in Texas, America, where she used to live, the land had been as flat as an ice rink and mostly reddish-orange with only a few boulders and cacti to break the monotony of the desert. When she first moved there from England some years ago, she had felt as if she was living on the set of a Wild West movie! She'd never forget the first time she saw cowboys in the street, wearing Stetson hats and riding skinny ponies with coils of rope looped over the saddle.

Coming back to England should have felt like coming home, but Andi had lived in London, and her mum's new job was in Aldcliffe, a suburb of Lancaster, not far from the Lake District. Real mountains loomed on the horizon, and Andi knew that vast slender lakes stretched between them, reflecting the hills and the skylike mirrors. The scenery here was as different from London as it was from Texas! Her mum had promised they could take a trip out to the lakes once they had finished unpacking and found their way round their new neighbourhood. But right now, when Andi didn't know which way to go next, that didn't seem likely to happen any time soon.

Above the mountains, the sky was dark with thick black clouds, so she walked faster, wanting to get home before it started to rain. Buddy trotted beside her on his lead, his stumpy tail wagging and his claws clicking lightly against the pavement. At the end of the street Andi looked in both directions, but all she could see were more rows of gold and scarlet trees stretching along the road.

"I wish we'd stayed in Texas, Bud," she sighed. It would still be hot enough to swim back there, even though it was September. She would probably be cooling off in her best friend Jess's swimming pool right now if her mum hadn't been offered a promotion in England.

Andi, her mum, and Buddy had arrived in Aldcliffe two days ago, on Friday. They'd flown from Texas direct to Manchester airport. All the way across the Atlantic, Andi had tried to convince herself that things would turn out all right once they arrived, but now that they were here, everything seemed to be going wrong.

Their new home was much smaller than their last one, which had been a sprawling single-storey with big rooms full of sunshine. This new house had three storeys. Andi's room was on the top floor, in the converted attic, with views of distant purple mountains. She'd liked the quirky shape of it when she'd first seen it, with its window set into the roof slope. But it had been empty then. Now it was crowded with packing crates, and Andi couldn't imagine ever making it look as good as her bedroom back in Texas.

The house had a neat garden with a lawn and flowerbeds, but after hours cooped up in the plane, she and Buddy had needed space to run. They'd come out in the hope of finding a park, but it had been nearly an hour and all they'd seen were roads and roads of houses.

The sky seemed to be growing darker by the minute. "There's a storm coming," Andi said with a shiver. She wasn't just worried about getting wet; Buddy was terrified of thunder, so she needed to get him indoors quickly.

She began to run, staring hopefully at each street sign, but even their names were confusing: Willow Walk, Weeping Willow Way, Beech Drive, Birch Grove . . .

Suddenly she had an idea. She'd heard stories of dogs leading their owners home when they were lost. Of course, Buddy had only just moved in too, but perhaps he had a better sense of direction than she had. Maybe he'd have some homing instinct that would lead him straight back to his basket, his favourite squeaky toy bone, and his food bowl. She wasn't sure it would work, but it was worth a try.

She unclipped Buddy's lead. "Home, Buddy! Find the way home, boy!"

Buddy barked excitedly and danced round in circles with his ears pricked. Then he lifted his head and shot off along the road.

"Wait for me, boy!" Andi cried, racing after him.

Buddy veered into a back alley and Andi felt a burst of hope. He really seemed to know where he was going! As she neared the entrance to the alley, she heard a mad scrabbling sound. Skidding round the corner, she saw a fat black-and-white cat clawing its way up a high fence. Buddy jumped at it and, resting his front paws halfway up the fence, began barking furiously.

"Buddy!" Andi scolded. "Leave that poor cat alone!"

Buddy stopped barking and dropped on to all four paws. He looked at Andi sheepishly, his tongue hanging out.

Andi couldn't help smiling. She'd really thought her plan was going to work, but it was obvious Buddy didn't know the way home at all. He'd just been chasing the cat!

The cat scrambled noisily to the top of the fence. It wobbled there for a few seconds, then dug its claws in and turned round to hiss at Buddy. A moment later it jumped down the other side. Buddy darted round the end of the fence and disappeared.

"Come back, Bud!" Andi called. She hurtled after him, worried that he might get lost without her. The top of the fence got lower as it ran further along the alley, and Andi could look over it to see a row of tidy gardens. The cat was stalking across a clipped lawn, swishing its tail angrily. But Buddy seemed to have forgotten all about it. He'd found a patch of mud at the edge of the grass and dived in for a good, long roll.

"Oh, Buddy!" Andi sighed. "Now I'll have to give you a bath." Normally she loved washing him, but that was back home – no, back in *Texas*, where there was a big garden room with a sink perfect for bathing little dogs. In her new house, she'd have to use the bathtub, and she didn't even know where Buddy's special shampoo was. Boxes were piled everywhere, waiting to be unpacked, and it could be in any one of them.

Buddy wriggled from side to side in the mud, beating his whippy tail on the ground. As Andi bent down to clip on his lead, he squirmed over on to his stomach, splashing her with mud. Andi groaned and tried to brush it off, but it just smeared over her jeans. Shrugging, she hurried along the alley.

They emerged into another unfamiliar street. Andi held tight to Buddy's lead. The storm clouds had sunk even lower, almost hiding the mountain peaks in the distance. "Which way now?" she wondered. Making up her mind, she turned left.

Halfway along the road, on the edge of a pretty garden, was a letterbox mounted on a post. It caught Andi's eye not just because it reminded her of the mailboxes in America, but because it was painted with an unusual design of turquoise peacock feathers. If she hadn't been worried that she'd never find the way home, Andi would have stopped to admire it.

She was carefully crossing another road when she noticed something that looked familiar. It was a lamppost with a dented SLOW sign fixed to it. Andi was sure there was one just like that on the bend before her new house!

She ran along the pavement with Buddy scampering beside her. He tried to catch the lead in his teeth as he ran, as if he thought this was one big game. They hurtled round the corner, and there was Andi's house, looking bare and unlived-in because there'd been no time to hang curtains yet. "We've made it, Buddy!" she gasped.

Their car wasn't parked outside, so Andi guessed her mum must still be at the corner shop. Luckily, their local shop stayed open late on Sundays, so Mrs Talbot had gone out to pick up some groceries before she started her new job, and Andi started at school, the next day. Andi unlocked the front door just as the first drops of rain began to fall. "Good timing, Buddy!" she exclaimed, laughing with relief. She unclipped his lead. "I'd better get you into the bath before Mum gets home."

Buddy scampered along the freshly-painted hall and into the living room, dodging a teetering stack of boxes, and leaving a trail of muddy footprints behind him. "No!" cried Andi. She ran after him and found him shaking himself right in the middle of the room. Splashes of mud flew off his fur and splattered the boxes and the living-room carpet.

"Bad Buddy!" Andi scolded.

He stopped shaking and trotted over to her with his ears pricked. Andi sighed and scooped him up. She couldn't get cross with him. He must be feeling as confused as she was about their new home. Keeping a tight hold on the little dog, Andi began to search for his shampoo. It was in the fourth box she tried, along with his towel, which was red with green paw prints. Andi pulled them out, then headed for the bathroom.

While she waited for the tub to fill, she stared

out of the window and thought wistfully of Texas. September storms were spectacular there, turning the sky lilac, pink and orange. Here, the rain-filled sky was grey, cold and miserable.

When the bath was ready, Andi took off Buddy's collar and laid it on the floor, out of splash range. Then she lifted him into the warm, foamy water. He stretched up to lick her cheek before sitting down with a splash.

"At least we still have each other, Bud," Andi murmured, stroking his head.

She had owned Buddy for a year, since he'd been a tiny puppy. Her mum and dad had taken her to the Animal Protection League to choose a dog, and he'd looked so lonely in his pen, all by himself, that she'd fallen in love with him at once – especially when he'd jumped onto her trainer and started chewing her shoelace. His brothers and sisters had been sold before him because he had a claw missing on his left front paw, but it never bothered him. It didn't bother Andi, either!

Soon after Buddy had moved in, Andi's parents told her they were splitting up. Though her dad was based in Texas, his work for an oil company took him all over the world, and even though he sent Andi postcards from all the places he went, it was hard not to miss him a lot. Buddy had helped keep Andi from feeling too upset when her dad went away, but even when he'd been at home in Texas, it had felt odd that he lived in a different house. And now they'd come back to Aldcliffe, not far from where her mum had grown up, it felt very strange to have left her dad on the other side of the world.

Sitting in the bathtub, up to his stomach in bubbles, Buddy ducked under a heap of lather and reappeared looking like a doggy version of Father Christmas with white hair and whiskers. Andi laughed and pulled out the bath plug, then switched on the shower hose to rinse Buddy's fur.

"That's it, Bud," she said when the last of the shampoo bubbles had been washed away. She lifted him out of the bath and wrapped him in his towel. He grunted happily and settled on her lap as she began to dry him.

She heard the front door open. "Hello, darling!" called her mum. "How did your walk go? Did you find a park?"

"No, not yet," Andi called back. "But I didn't look

too far. I didn't want to get lost." She decided not to tell her mum that she very nearly hadn't found her way home.

Judy Talbot came upstairs and into the bathroom. Her curly, brown hair was wet with rain. "Maybe we'll go out next weekend and find a good place to walk Buddy. Have you given him a bath?"

"Yes. He rolled in some mud and got filthy."

Andi's mum laughed. "Typical Buddy!" She ruffled his damp fur. "He looks pretty happy, mind you."

He gave a little bark, as though to tell her she was right.

"Good for you, Buddy," Mrs Talbot said. She straightened up. "I'm just going to bring the shopping in from the car, then I'll think about supper." She went downstairs again.

Andi finished rubbing Buddy dry. "We'll find a park soon, Bud," she promised.

Buddy licked her nose.

Suddenly, a flash of lightning filled the bathroom with silver light. It was followed by a deafening roll and clap of thunder that sounded like a boulder falling on the house. Buddy yelped, then shot out of the bathroom and down the stairs.

"Come back!" Andi called, darting after him. "It's OK, Bud!"

As Andi reached the bottom stair, the front door opened and her mum came in with several bags of shopping. Buddy streaked along the hall towards her.

"Stop him!" Andi yelled.

Her mum threw down the carrier bags and made a grab for Buddy, but she wasn't quick enough. The small furry shape wriggled past her, his claws scrabbling on the floor, and darted out into the rainy street.

"Buddy!" Andi shouted. She raced along the hall, leapt over the bags of shopping, and sped outside. Buddy was charging away down the pavement, his ears flat and his paws kicking up puddle water behind him. As the rain came down harder, he faded into the distance until he was little more than a smudgy brown-and-white blur.

"Buddy, come back!" Andi tore after him, her heartbeat thudding in her ears. She had to catch him! They'd been lost before when they'd been out

14

together, so what chance would Buddy have of finding his way home when he was by himself?

More lightning fizzed across the sky, lighting up the street in a steely-white glare. The clap of thunder that followed made Buddy shrink down, flattening his belly to the ground, but somehow he kept running. A moment later, he disappeared round the corner at the end of the street. Andi ran faster than she had ever run before, but by the time she reached the corner, the little dog had vanished.

Chapter Two

Andi ran through the pouring rain, calling Buddy's name. She had to find him, she just had to! But where could she look? She'd already been lost once today. She tried to memorize road names as she sped along, so she'd be able to find her way back when she found Buddy. *If* she found him . . .

On and on she raced, scanning the gardens on either side of the road. She hadn't stopped to grab a jacket on her way out and she was soon soaking wet, but she didn't care. All that mattered was finding Buddy. But she was panting too hard to call his name now and her chest ached. Her legs were so wobbly they felt like they were made of jelly, and she was forced to slow down to a jog before she fell over.

A woman was hurrying along the road in the opposite direction, pushing a buggy with one hand and holding a huge umbrella in the other.

"Did a Jack Russell run past you?" Andi asked, panting.

The woman shook her head. "Sorry, I haven't seen any dogs."

Andi began to retrace her steps. She'd been running so fast that she might have gone straight past Buddy. Perhaps he'd been hiding under a bush in a stranger's garden, whimpering with fear. Perhaps he was watching the street right now, waiting for her to come back and get him.

The thunder had faded away, growling in the distance like a bad-tempered bear, but the rain kept pelting down. Andi reached another road that she didn't recognize and turned into it. It was lined with more large, lush trees that blocked her view of the houses. She jogged along the street, peering into the gardens.

The houses eventually grew further and further apart until they stopped altogether. To her astonishment, Andi found herself standing at the edge of a vast fruit orchard that stretched on and on until it was swallowed up by the grey sky. The leaves on the branches shuddered as the rain lashed down, and now and then an apple was broken free by the wind and dropped with a thud. Andi could hardly believe that she lived so close to the edge of town. Why hadn't she and Buddy found this orchard on their walk? *Not that it's any good for walking dogs*, she told herself. It was fenced off, and the farmer was hardly likely to welcome them tramping through his field. But if they were this close to the edge of town, there might be some woods nearby where Buddy could have gone for shelter.

"Buddy!" Andi yelled. "Are you in there?" Perhaps he'd squeezed under the lowest strand of the wire fence and scampered in among the trees.

There was no answering bark.

"Buddy!" she called again. "Here, boy!" She scanned the orchard, searching for a small, darting shape, but it was hard to see clearly. Raindrops splashing in her eyes made her blink, and the light was fading quickly.

Before long, Andi's hair and clothes were stuck to her skin, and her trainers felt as if they were filling up with water. She called for ages, growing more and more anxious. What if Buddy was lost among the fruit trees and never found his way out? Like all Jack Russells, there was nothing Buddy enjoyed more than a rabbit chase, and with so much grass, the orchard was probably home to hundreds of them.

At last, when the daylight was nothing but a narrow band of pale grey on the horizon, Andi realized it was hopeless. If Buddy was in the orchard, he wasn't coming out. And if he wasn't in there, then he could be just about anywhere.

Shivering, Andi squeezed the worst of the rainwater from her hair and set off home, her trainers squelching with every step. The streetlights had come on, making the puddles gleam like pools of spilled orange juice all along the street. The curtains were drawn in most of the houses and the pavements were empty. Andi trudged along, hoping she was making all the right turns. From time to time, she stopped to call out, "Buddy!" But there was never a familiar bark in reply, just the endless rattle of raindrops on the streets and roofs and cars.

Suddenly, a square shape loomed up ahead, exotically swirled with green and blue. It was the peacock-feather letterbox! Now Andi knew exactly where she was. She sped up. Maybe Buddy had come home while she'd been out looking for him.

A few moments later she was passing the dented SLOW sign, and then she could see her house. Lights blazed from the bare windows. Andi raced across the sodden grass to the front door and burst inside. "Is Buddy home?"

Her mum came out of the kitchen, shaking her head. She was drying her hands on a towel. "No, darling. I'm sorry. I phoned the RSPCA and the police while you were out, just in case he'd been handed in, but they haven't seen him."

"What am I going to do?" Andi gasped, suddenly close to tears.

"Well, why don't we drive round and try to spot him?" Mrs Talbot suggested.

"Yes! What are we waiting for?" As Andi turned towards the door again, her mum handed her the towel.

"Dry your hair in the car, Andi. You're soaked."

They drove slowly along the neighbouring streets, Andi pressing her face to the window as she peered out. Her spirits started to sink again. It was

completely dark now and there were too many patches of shadows where Buddy could be hiding.

"I'm sorry. This isn't going to work," her mum said sympathetically, after they'd been driving for about twenty minutes. She pulled over and squeezed Andi's hand. "Let's call it a night, love. Maybe Buddy will find his own way home. After all, he knows the neighbourhood from your walk this afternoon. And if he doesn't come back, we'll leave for school extra early tomorrow so we can look for him on the way."

Andi knew her mum was right. There was no way they'd find him in the dark.

They had pizza followed by strawberry ice cream for supper – Andi's favourite – but she was too anxious to eat. She sat at the table, surrounded by boxes, listening for Buddy's bark outside.

"He'll be all right," Mrs Talbot said. "I bet he's found somewhere warm and dry to sleep, like that time he got lost when he was a puppy and turned up in the airing cupboard."

Andi tried to smile but then she spotted Buddy's bowls on the kitchen floor. They were both empty — there was no point putting out Bud's favourite meat and biscuits if he wasn't there to eat it. Andi looked away hurriedly, and her gaze fell on a "Happy Moving" card from Jessica Martin, her best friend back in Texas.

"I wish I could email Jess," she said. Jess loved Buddy too, and she'd be really sad to hear that he was missing.

"I'll try and get the computer set up tomorrow," said Mrs Talbot, "so you can email her after school."

A chilling thought struck Andi. What if Buddy didn't realize they'd come to England on a plane? He'd been shut in a special dog carrier for the journey and he might think he could walk all the way back to their old home in Texas! The idea of such a tiny dog setting out on such an impossible journey was terrifying. He could end up anywhere!

Andi lay in bed, tossing and turning, listening for the bark that would tell her Buddy was home. Her bed felt cold and lonely without him lying in the crook of her knees, and she missed his steady breathing as he slept.

Time and time again, she slipped out of bed and

peered out at the empty street, straining her eyes to catch a glimpse of Buddy's white-and-tan fur in the dim light from the streetlights. Each time she climbed into bed again, her head whirled with images of all the bad things that could be happening to her dog.

"I miss you so much, Buddy," she whispered into the darkness, feeling tears well up in her eyes. What if he never came home? What if she never saw him again? The tears spilled over, pouring down her cheeks, and Andi cried for a long time before she finally fell asleep.

Chapter Three

The first faint streaks of dawn were stretching across the sky when Andi got up the next morning. She ran straight downstairs and opened the front door to look up and down the street. There was still no sign of Buddy.

Miserably, she went back upstairs. Her mum had left her new school uniform draped over a chair in her bedroom. There was a navy sweatshirt and a matching skirt. Andi put it aside and pulled on an old sweatshirt, worried that Buddy might not recognize her in anything new.

Andi could hear her mum in the shower, so she thought she must have at least an hour before they needed to leave. Good — that would give her just enough time to have another quick look for Buddy.

It had stopped raining, but the pavement was dotted with puddles. Andi set off in the direction Buddy had taken the night before. The sky was pale grey, with a pink tinge along the horizon where the sun would soon come up. Aldcliffe was beginning to stir, with curtains being drawn back like sleepy eyes opening. A few cars sped by, their tyres hissing on the wet road.

A paperboy shot past on his bike. He was wearing a baseball cap and a blue hooded sweatshirt.

"Hang on!" Andi called, running after him.

He stopped and waited for her to catch up, nodding his head to a rhythm that Andi couldn't hear. As she drew near, she saw that he was listening to an Ipod clipped to the belt of his jeans. He was older than she'd thought, fourteen or fifteen maybe, with red hair and cute blue eyes. Andi suddenly felt shy.

"What's up?" he asked, slipping his headphones down round his neck.

Andi took a deep breath. "I've lost my dog. A tan-and-white Jack Russell terrier. Have you seen him?"

The boy shook his head. "No, sorry." He put his headphones on again and placed one foot on a pedal, ready to ride away.

"Wait!" said Andi. "Let me give you my phone number in case you see him, OK? Have you got anything to write on?"

The boy reached into his bag and tore a blank corner off a newspaper. "Here."

Andi fished in her pocket. She was sure she had a pen in there from when she and her mum had played a game on the plane. She held the scrap of paper and tried to remember her new phone number, but for a moment all she could think of was her old one in Texas.

The paperboy looked at his watch. "I've gotta go," he said, "or I'll be late for school. I've still got loads of papers to deliver."

"No, wait." To Andi's relief, the number popped into her head. She scribbled it down and pushed the piece of paper into the boy's hand. "You will call if you see him? Please?"

"Yeah, sure." He put it in his pocket and rode away with his headphones back in his ears.

Andi hurried on. She was glad that the paperboy

had taken her number, but she wasn't sure he'd notice Buddy with his headphones on.

Halfway down the next street, she reached a narrow alley lined with dustbins – another place Buddy might have chosen to hide if he was frightened. She called his name and stood on tiptoe to peer over the fences on either side, but there was no sign of him, and soon she was out in the street again. *I'm not giving up*, she told herself. Buddy was out here somewhere and she was going to find him. She looked under parked cars and bushes, and behind hedges, but he was nowhere to be seen.

As she turned another corner on to a street of large houses set back from the road, she spotted a postman ahead. He was jogging between each house and Andi had to rush to catch up with him. "Excuse me!" she panted.

He turned, smiling and jogging on the spot, his postbag bouncing against his hip. "Hey!" he said happily. He was in his early twenties, and he was tall and lean with long, black dreadlocked hair tied back in a ponytail. Andi noticed that he was wearing a pair of well-worn athletic trainers.

"I'm training for the London Marathon," he

explained, following her gaze. To her surprise, he wasn't even out of breath. "I'm writing a book about it, too: *Mad Mike Morgan's Marathon Manual*. And I'm Mike Morgan, the fastest postman in Lancashire, at your service."

"I'm Andi Talbot." She held out her hand to him.

"Talbot, Talbot," Mike muttered. "Oh yeah, 20 Aspen Drive." Still jogging, he shook her hand, then delved into his bag. "These are for you." He pulled out a handful of letters. "Do you want them now or should I put them through your letterbox?"

"Through the letterbox, please." Andi might have to carry Buddy if he was tired when she found him – or worse, hurt. She didn't want to be holding letters as well. "I'm looking for my Jack Russell terrier, Buddy. Have you seen him?"

Mike stopped his jogging and looked serious for a moment. "I'm not much of a dog lover. You know how dogs feel about postmen, don't you? Well, seems that's the case with me, at least. They're always barking at me for some reason. But I'll keep an eye out, and I'll ask everyone back at the post office to watch out for him, too."

"Thanks!" Andi began to feel a little better.

Everyone was being so helpful; surely Buddy would turn up soon. "You don't need to be afraid of Buddy," she told Mike. "He's never bitten anyone in his life. Ever."

"Good to know. All right, good luck on your dog hunt!" Mike jogged on to the next house.

Andi spotted a playground on the other side of the road then, and crossed over for a closer look. Buddy had always loved walking along the beach in Texas, and she hoped she might spot his paw prints in the sandpit. But the sand was smooth and flat, marked only by hundreds of tiny raindrop holes. Buddy wasn't curled up under the slide or the monkey bars either.

Andi began to feel anxious again. She was running out of time. She ran to the end of the street and stared round at the unfamiliar houses. "I really, really wish we'd never moved to Aldcliffe!" she said out loud.

Discouraged, she made her way to a corner shop she'd noticed on the other side of the street. The door was propped open, and there was a short blonde woman bustling about behind the counter. Andi needed directions back to Aspen Drive, so she went into the shop. The shelves were crammed with colourful cans and packets, from noodles to hot chocolate. Andi's stomach rumbled loudly and she realized she was starving. She fished inside her pockets as she approached the counter, but she had come out empty-handed. She also realized that she wasn't wearing her watch. As well as Andi getting to school, her mum was starting her new job today, and they had to be on time.

"Hello." The woman greeted Andi with a friendly smile.

Andi smiled back. "Hi! Could you tell me the time, please?"

The woman glanced at her watch. "Twenty past eight."

"Oh, no!" Andi gasped.

"Late for something?" the woman guessed.

"I'm new here," Andi explained. "My mum and I moved to Aspen Drive yesterday and now I'm lost."

"Are you Judy Talbot's daughter?"

"Er, yes." Andi stared at the woman in amazement. How on earth did she know that?

The woman laughed. "Don't look so surprised, dear. Your mum called yesterday to see what sort of dog food we stocked. I'm Rachel Brand, by the way."

"I'm Andi, and I've lost my dog, Buddy, a Jack Russell. Have you seen him?"

Rachel's smile faded. "Oh, Andi! That's terrible. And in your first week in Aldcliffe! Well, if it helps at all, this is a very friendly town – I'm sure your little dog will be found before long. I'll check my storeroom, just in case he's crept inside, and I'll ask all my customers to keep an eye out for him, too. If anyone spots the little chap, I'll let you know. I'll ask Dean to look for him, too. He's my paperboy."

Andi felt a bit dazed as she listened to Rachel talk at top speed. "Thanks. And, um, could you tell me how to get home from here?"

"Of course, it's not far. Your road's the next one on the left." Rachel pressed a muesli bar into Andi's hand. "There you go. This'll keep your strength up if you don't have time for breakfast."

"Thank you!" Andi said again. She smiled, feeling as if she'd just made her first friend in Aldcliffe. Maybe Rachel was right – in a place this friendly, Buddy couldn't stay lost forever!

* * *

Mrs Talbot came hurrying out of the kitchen when Andi got home. She was dressed in her grey business suit and a cream blouse. "Andi, where have you been? We have to leave in ten minutes!"

"I was looking for Buddy. I'm sorry I'm late, but I got lost."

"Any sign of him?"

"No, but I ran into a few people who promised to look out for him."

Her mum squeezed her shoulder. "That's great, love. We'll find him, I'm sure of it. Now hurry up and get changed for school. If you're quick, there should be time to search a few streets on the way. And if we don't find him before school, I'm sure he'll turn up later."

"I hope you're right," Andi said quietly before she headed upstairs.

Chapter Four

Andi gazed hopefully out of the car window as her mum reversed out of the driveway. They drove slowly up one street and down another, but there was no sign of any dogs at all, let alone a tan-and-white Jack Russell.

"Oh, no!" Mrs Talbot exclaimed, stopping abruptly.

"What's wrong?" Andi asked.

"I've gone the wrong way. I should have turned left at the last corner." She turned the car round. "The trouble is, every road here looks the same with all these trees. And it's so different to how it was when I was a girl."

"I know what you mean about the trees!" Andi agreed. "I thought I'd never get back yesterday. But now I find my way by the SLOW sign and the peacock letterbox."

"Good thinking," her mum said approvingly. "It's great to know you're already spotting landmarks to help you find your way around. It won't be long before you feel like you've lived here forever."

Andi nodded and stared out of the window again. Maybe the neighbourhood was starting to feel a bit more familiar, but she didn't want to stay here for another minute if she didn't have Buddy.

Fairfield Middle School was a two-storey, flat-roofed building, about half the size of Andi's old school in Texas. There were large playing fields behind the school, though, which caught Andi's eye as soon as her mum pulled in to the kerb. She was looking forward to her first games lesson there – she loved sports, especially athletics. But thinking about the playing fields reminded her of Buddy. He'd love all that grass to run around on.

Andi tried to remember everything her mum had told her about the school, in an attempt to take her mind off her dog. She didn't want to start crying when she'd have to face her classmates in a few minutes. She'd never even visited the school before but her mum had looked round when she'd flown over to England to sort out the details of her new job and to look for a house. Andi remembered that the headteacher was called Miss Cranmer and that her classroom would be on the ground floor. Now, seeing Fairfield for the first time, Andi felt a surge of homesickness. She had a sudden crazy wish that her mum would say it was all a mistake and that they'd be heading back to Texas just as soon as they'd found Buddy.

"Here we are," Mrs Talbot said. "Are you sure you don't want me to come in with you?"

"Mum! I'm not a baby! Good luck at your new job!" Andi gave her mum a kiss, then climbed out of the car. She felt so nervous, she thought her legs would crumple underneath her and she'd end up in a heap on the pavement.

"Thanks, but I don't need luck – they're going to love me today, just like the kids at this school will love you," Mrs Talbot said. She flashed Andi an encouraging smile and drove away.

Wishing the butterflies in her stomach would settle down, Andi held her head high and tried to look confident. Then she shouldered her backpack and joined the other students moving into the playground. They all looked older than her, and she wondered if the other Year Fives had already gone in.

Suddenly, Andi heard someone say, "Look! That's the girl who lost her dog." She spun round, wondering who could possibly know about Buddy. Just behind her, the paperboy with the cute eyes was leaning out of a car window. A younger boy was getting out of the back seat. He had red hair and a face so freckly that it reminded Andi of a speckled pebble. He looked about the same height as Andi and she wondered whether he was in Year Five too.

"Hi," he said, grinning so broadly that his grey eyes crinkled. He walked over to Andi and dumped his rucksack on the ground. "Dean told me about your dog. Has he turned up?"

Andi shook her head, suddenly feeling shy. It didn't help when Dean smiled at her. "Good luck on your first day," he said. "See you later, Tris." He closed the window and the car pulled away from the kerb.

"I'm Tristan," the younger boy went on, grinning at Andi. "That was my brother. What's your name?"

"Andi," she said, smiling back.

"This is your first day at Fairfield, right? Dean told me you were new to the area."

Andi nodded. "Yes, I've just moved here from Texas."

The boy's grin grew even wider. "Texas! You didn't bring a couple of dolphins in your suitcase, did you? I've always wanted to swim with dolphins."

Andi grinned back. "Sorry, they wouldn't fit," she joked. She looked round the playground, hoping everyone would be as friendly as Tristan. It was packed with kids, running and shouting and rifling through their rucksacks. Maybe one of them had seen Buddy, but there was no way she could ask them all.

"Hey, come on. I'll show you round," Tristan said. He led Andi into the crowd of people piling towards the main doors. Before they were inside, he raised his voice and stretched out his arms. "As you see, we have an impressively smooth, spacious playground with state-of-the-art recreation facilities," he announced dramatically.

Andi laughed. "Wow, this is some guided tour!"

Tristan smiled at her and explained, "My mum and dad are estate agents. You should hear some of the things they say when they describe houses they have to sell!" The crowd of kids narrowed down as they approached the doors. "Here we have the school itself, a roomy building – light and welcoming – equipped with the very latest in educational equipment."

Still laughing, Andi followed him into the reception area, which had a polished wood floor and a high ceiling. Several offices were there, two corridors led off in different directions, and a flight of stairs rose to the first floor. Beside them, just inside the main door, was an enormous notice board fastened to the wall. A poster advertising trials for the football team caught Andi's eye and she stopped to read it. She loved football. "Are you going to try out for the team?" she asked Tristan.

He shrugged. "I'll probably have to. My dad is a sports nut and he's desperate for me to get on to a school team. I don't stand a chance, though. I can never get my arms and legs to work together when there's a ball around." He made a sudden lunge for an imaginary ball and collided with a teacher who was passing with an armful of maths books.

The teacher staggered back with a gasp and the books flew up in the air, landing with a thud and a flutter of pages. "Tristan Saunders, what on earth do you think you're doing?" she exclaimed.

"Sorry, Mrs Manning. I didn't know you were there." Tristan scrambled for the books and Andi knelt down to help him. They stacked them in a tidy pile, then Tristan handed them back to the teacher.

Looking flustered, Mrs Manning took the books and swept on along the corridor.

Tristan waited until she'd gone, then burst out laughing. "Phew! That was lucky! It might have been Miss Ashworthy! She's much worse."

Andi hoped she wouldn't have Miss Ashworthy or Mrs Manning for any classes. "Are any of the teachers here nice?" she asked.

"Lots of them, but Miss Ashworthy wins the scary teacher prize and Mrs Manning's a close second. The rest aren't bad. Mr Wallace, the football coach, is great. He never points out how useless I am, no matter how many times I fall over."

"I'll help you practise if you want to get into the team," Andi offered, "though it might be better if we do it outside. Buddy makes a great defender . . ." She broke off, suddenly feeling sad, and stepped away from the notice board. How could she even think about football when poor Buddy was missing?

"Is Buddy your dog?" Tristan asked.

She nodded.

"We should make posters so everyone knows Buddy's lost," he suggested.

Andi glanced back at the colourful notice board. Two boys had come in from the playground and were looking at the football poster. Maybe Tristan was right. If a poster of Buddy was pinned up there, people would be sure to see it. "Let's do it," she said. Hope began to bubble up inside her again.

"I wish I'd thought of it before," Tristan sighed. "I lost my cat, Lucy, about three months ago."

"Didn't you put up posters for her, then?"

He shook his head and a look of sadness flashed across his face. "No. If I had, someone might have found her and got in touch."

"Isn't she microchipped?" Andi asked.

"Microchipped?" Tristan echoed, not really understanding.

"Haven't you heard of it? A vet injects a tiny numbered chip underneath your pet's skin, just on the neck. It doesn't hurt at all. Then the number's put into a computer with your name and address, so when the animal's scanned by any vet, they can tell who owns it. I had Buddy done ages ago."

"What a great idea!" Tristan cried. "I wish Lucy'd had one of those. Is it expensive to have the chip put in?"

"No, well not in America, anyway. You do have microchips here, don't you?" she asked, suddenly anxious. If somebody found Buddy they might take him to the vet, but what if nobody thought to check for a chip?

"Yeah. I'd sort of heard of it, but I didn't know what it was." Tristan looked sad again. "I just wish we'd done it for Lucy before she disappeared."

"You must really miss her," Andi said sympathetically.

"Yes," agreed Tristan. Then his face brightened. "I like to think that she's found a nice new owner.

44

I just hope they've discovered her favourite food is anchovies."

"Buddy likes sausages best. But I don't want him to find a new owner," Andi added hastily. She couldn't bear the thought of that! "Come on," she said. "Let's work out what we're going to write on the posters." She had to give Aldcliffe a chance to be as friendly as Texas, and let as many people as possible know that a very special dog was missing!

Chapter Five

Before Tristan had a chance to reply, the bell rang. "I'll meet you in the library at lunchtime," he said. "We can talk about the posters then."

"What about your friends?" asked Andi. "Don't you usually have lunch with them?"

"They won't mind – in any case, they'll soon be your friends, too! Right now, I'll do whatever it takes to help you get your dog back. I know what it's like to lose a pet. So, we'll need paper, pens, photos . . ." He began ticking them off on his fingers. "Wow. This list is going to be so long we'll need a suitcase to carry everything."

Andi grinned. Tristan's knack for comedy was making her feel more positive about finding Buddy.

People began to swarm down the corridors on

either side of the staircase. "Whose class are you in?" Tristan asked.

"Mr Dixon's."

Tristan pointed along the left corridor. "Down here, third door on the left. I'll have to drop you off at the door because my teacher's Miss Ashworthy – and she's even scarier if you're late."

Andi followed him along the corridor, suddenly wishing that they were in the same class. He stopped outside a bright-green door. "Here you go." He shot off in the opposite direction. "See you at lunchtime!" he called over his shoulder. "The library's on the first floor!"

Andi felt very alone as she watched him disappear into the crowd. Taking a deep breath, she stepped into the classroom. Her new classmates were already sitting at their desks. Some were scribbling in notebooks, while others were chatting, but they all stopped talking and turned to stare at her when she appeared. Andi felt herself go bright red as she made her way to Mr Dixon's desk. She felt awkward and clumsy, as though her feet had suddenly grown ten sizes.

"You must be our new girl," Mr Dixon said,

beaming at her. "Andi Talbot from Texas. Glad to meet you, Andi."

"Thanks." There was a lump in her throat the size of Alaska. She tried to swallow it, but it was stuck firmly. Fixing a smile on her face, she looked round at her classmates. There were no answering smiles. Some were still staring and some had returned to their conversations. A tall girl with a long blonde plait looked up from a magazine she was reading with her friend. "You might have trouble putting her in a group if she's from Texas, sir," she suggested, loud enough for the whole class to hear. "She might not have seen the sea before."

Everyone laughed and Andi's cheeks flared again.

"Thank you, Natalie, but Andi used to live in England, so I think she'll be perfectly familiar with the concept of oceans. We're studying sea life this term," Mr Dixon explained to Andi. "Each group is investigating a different sea creature for our science and environmental project." He looked round the room. "There's a space over there." He pointed to a table near the back of the class, where two girls and two boys were sitting.

Andi walked over to them and sat in the empty chair, placing her rucksack on her lap. She smiled shyly and was relieved when the others smiled back. "Which sea creatures are you studying?" she asked.

"Squid and jellyfish," said one of the boys. "Howard and I have been finding out what they eat, and Kelly and Larissa are making a map of where different species live. I'm Chen, by the way."

"Is there anything I can do?" Andi offered.

The four of them looked at each other. "You could help with the map," one of the girls said. "There's not much left to do now. A bit of colouring, that's all."

"OK," said Andi. She unzipped her rucksack to look for her crayons.

"Now settle down," said Mr Dixon. "I've got some important announcements before we take the register."

Everyone stopped talking and turned to look at him. "First, the playing field is out of bounds today. It's soaked after all that rain yesterday, and Miss Cranmer doesn't want it to turn into a swamp."

Andi looked out of the window, the memory of

yesterday's storm filling her mind – all that rain and scary thunder. Somewhere out there, Buddy was on his own. He'd be so frightened – if only she could find him!

"Andi," Mr Dixon called.

Andi jumped and spun round, knocking her pencil case on to the floor.

The teacher smiled, but there was a tiny frown between his eyes. "Pay attention, please. I've called your name three times already."

A few people giggled and Andi turned even redder than before. "Sorry," she said, bending down to pick up her crayons. Larissa bent down to help, flashing Andi a sympathetic smile.

After the register had been taken, the class worked on their projects. Andi helped to colour the jellyfish map. Larissa and Kelly were obviously good friends – they were talking about a sleepover they'd been to over the weekend. Howard and Chen were arguing good-naturedly about last night's football match. Andi couldn't help feeling left out.

When she'd finished colouring her section of the map, she picked up a book about jellyfish and flipped through it. It was hard to concentrate because she kept wondering where Buddy was. Soon she found herself gazing miserably out of the window again. "Hang in there, Bud," she whispered. "I'll find you soon, I promise."

The morning passed quickly: Andi was surprised when the bell rang for lunch. Even though she didn't feel as if she'd made any new best friends, she'd enjoyed all her lessons so far.

She leapt up, eager to get to the library and start planning the posters with Tristan. She hurried along the corridor and up the stairs to the library.

Andi soon found herself in a spacious room lined with tall bookshelves and with ceiling-high windows along one side. In the centre of the room, tables had been pushed together, some with computers. The windows looked out across the playing fields. Andi scanned them quickly for a familiar tan-and-white shape, but they were empty.

Tristan was sitting at a table with his back to the windows, surrounded by sheets of paper. "Over here, Andi!" he called in a loud whisper. "I've made a list of all the things we'll need for the posters."

Feeling more hopeful than she had all morning, Andi ran to see. The list was very long: paper, thick marker pens in different colours, photos of Buddy, glue, drawing pins . . .

"My pocket money will never cover all that," she sighed, sinking into a chair.

"I didn't think of that," said Tristan, frowning.

A printer whirred to life beside them, making him jump.

"That's it!" Andi exclaimed. "We don't need to buy all that stuff for making posters by hand! We can design the posters on my computer at home, and print them in colour! I've taken loads of photos of Buddy with our digital camera. It'll be easy to paste one into a poster."

Tristan's eyebrows raised so high, they nearly vanished into his hair. "So are you good with computer graphics, then?" he asked, sounding impressed. "I only play games and surf the Internet on mine."

Andi nodded. "I love doing things with layout and colour. My old teacher, Miss Steadman, let me make a giant mural for the classroom on the computer."

The library door opened then, and the blonde girl who'd made the joke about Andi not knowing what an ocean was came in. To Andi's surprise, she walked straight over to them. "Don't they eat in Texas?" the girl demanded.

Andi stared at her, trying to remember her name. She thought Mr Dixon had called her Natalie, but she wasn't sure. "I didn't skip lunch," she explained. "I'm going down to the hall in a minute."

The girl shook her head. "You're too late. Didn't you hear Mr Dixon say that there's a training course in the hall for some of the teachers this afternoon? He told us before he took the register this morning. Lunch has finished already."

Andi felt her shoulders droop. Mr Dixon must have mentioned it while she was staring out of the window. Now she was starving. All she'd had to eat today was the muesli bar that Rachel had given her, and she hadn't eaten much last night either because she'd been so upset about losing Buddy.

The blonde girl shrugged as if to say it wasn't her problem and went over to the shelves to choose a book.

"Just my luck," Andi groaned.

"Sorry, I should have warned you about lunch," said Tristan. "I thought you might have brought a sandwich." He opened his lunch box. "Don't worry, you can share mine, if you want. Tuna."

"Ughh. Thanks, but no thanks," Andi said.

"You can have my crisps then. And half my banana."

Andi was grateful to Tristan for being so generous, but while she ate, all she could think about was Buddy. He must be really hungry by now, and Andi doubted whether he'd found anyone to share lunch with him.

Tristan offered to come home with Andi after school so they could start designing the posters. "I can show you the quickest way to walk home too," he said. "If you have estate agents for parents, you soon get to know every street and shortcut inside out and back to front!"

"Thanks, that would be great," Andi replied.

The afternoon passed even faster than the morning, and as soon as the last bell rang, Andi grabbed her rucksack and hurried out of the classroom to find Tristan.

They talked about the posters as they walked home, trying to think of the best wording to attract people's attention.

When they were a few streets from the school, a small tan-and-white shape hurtled out of a garden ahead of them. It was a Jack Russell terrier!

"Buddy!" Andi gasped, clutching Tristan's arm. "Quick! We've got to catch him!"

Chapter Six

"Buddy! Here, boy!" Andi called excitedly.

The little dog didn't seem to hear. He darted across the road and raced into an alley.

"Where's he going?" Andi wondered out loud. She and Tristan crossed the road carefully, then shot after the dog, their rucksacks bouncing on their shoulders.

"Buddy, come back!" Andi shouted.

As they raced into the alley, they saw the little dog nearing the other end. "Buddy!" yelled Andi. "Buddy! Stop!"

The dog slowed for a moment and looked back, but then dashed away again, disappearing round a corner.

Andi ran along the alley, jumping puddles and

dodging dustbins, with Tristan hard on her heels. Her heart was hammering. Why hadn't Buddy come to her? Had spending a night outdoors damaged his memory? Surely he couldn't have forgotten her in such a short time?

They burst out of the alley just in time to see the little Jack Russell heading for a kids' playground on the edge of a small park. He was trotting now, rather than running, and his tail was wagging excitedly.

Andi sped up. "Buddy!" she shouted breathlessly. "Here, boy!"

Still the dog didn't look round. He reached the playground gate and trotted inside.

The playground wasn't very big. It contained a few swings, a slide, and a seesaw. A girl of about seven was standing at the top of the slide. The dog scurried to the foot of the steps and barked at her.

"What's he doing?" asked Tristan, stopping in the gateway to get his breath back.

"Maybe he thinks that girl will give him a treat?" Andi suggested. "You wait here, Tristan, in case he tries to run out, and I'll go and catch him." She raced across the pavement, calling Buddy's name, overjoyed at the thought of taking her dog home again.

The little girl said something to the dog that Andi couldn't hear. Then she came whizzing down the slide. When she reached the bottom, the dog jumped into her arms and licked her face delightedly.

"What are you doing here, Scamp?" the little girl laughed. "Did you sneak out again?"

Andi stopped running, shocked. Had this girl already adopted Buddy and given him a new name? She was about to march up to the girl and tell her Buddy wasn't hers, when she realized that both of the dog's ears were completely tan. Buddy's left ear was white at the tip. Andi looked at the dog more closely, and now she could see that it was slightly smaller than Buddy and that its face was thinner, too. It wasn't Buddy at all! They'd been following the wrong dog.

Disappointment pressed down on her, making her rucksack feel like it was full of rocks. Andi had been so sure that this was *her* dog! Struggling not to cry, she turned away and headed back to the gate.

"What's up?" Tristan asked, running to meet her. "Where's your dog?"

Andi wasn't sure that she could trust herself to speak without bursting into tears.

"Isn't it him?" Tristan said gently.

Biting her trembling lip, Andi shook her head. "No," she whispered. She felt her shoulders slump. "Oh, Tristan, where is he?"

Tristan thought for a moment. "Well, he's a friendly dog, right?"

Andi nodded.

"In that case, maybe he's been here already, looking for someone to play with?" he suggested.

Andi stared at him, trying not to feel too hopeful. "Maybe." She looked round the playground and felt her shoulders sag. "But how would we know?" she asked in a small voice.

"Paw prints, of course," said Tristan confidently. Before Andi could point out that even the heaviest dog in the world wouldn't leave paw prints on pavement or grass, he hoisted his rucksack further onto his shoulder and started marching across the playground towards the far corner. When they had nearly reached the hedge, he stopped and pointed at an orange square set in the ground.

"A sandpit!" Andi cried. She ran past Tristan and crouched down to look at a trail of paw prints running right across the sand.

"They look about the right size," Tristan remarked, crouching down beside her. He frowned. "Although I don't think we'll really be able to tell if they belong to Buddy or that other terrier."

"No, wait, I can tell!" Andi exclaimed excitedly. She peered closer, and touched the nearest paw print with the tip of her finger. "They *are* his!" she whooped. "Look here – this print's got a missing claw!" she pointed out. "Buddy was born with a claw missing from his left front paw, so his prints look different from other dogs'."

"Good old Buddy, leaving a trail for us!" said Tristan. "The prints only seem to go one way, so maybe he went through the hedge." He straightened up and walked round the sandpit. There was a tiny gap at the bottom of the hedge on the far side. A few strands of tan-and-white fur were caught on the twigs round the hole. Andi leant down and peered through the hole into a narrow

alley enclosed by a high stone wall. "Buddy!" she
called. "Here, boy. Here, Buddy!"

"I'll go through and see if he's there," Tristan said.
He flung down his rucksack, then lay down and
wriggled into the hole. "Wow, it's smaller than it
looks," he puffed. "Andi, do you think you could go
round to the other side and give me a hand here? I
might be stuck."

"I'll see if I can find another way into the
alley," Andi said. She snatched up Tristan's
rucksack and sped out of the playground and
along the street. Soon she came to a narrow
opening between two houses. Diving into it, she
ran between high walls, calling Buddy's name.
As she rounded a corner, she saw Tristan's freckled
face looking up at her from the ground. There
were several leaves in his hair, and he looked
rather flustered.

Trying not to laugh, Andi grabbed hold of
his shoulders and heaved him through the
hedge. Tristan pushed himself to his feet and
brushed down his clothes, which were covered
with bits of twig. "I wonder where he went next?"
he said.

Andi looked down at the ground. It wasn't sandy here, but there was something else to give them a clue. "Look!" she said.

Beside the hedge was a muddy puddle. On the other side of it, dirty paw prints led off into the alley. "You can see where the claw's missing!" Tristan exclaimed, looking closer. "We must be on Buddy's trail."

They followed the trail round another corner and into a paved courtyard. A door stood open on the far side, and they could hear voices and the clatter of saucepans being crashed around. A sign beside the door read:

VIALLI'S RESTAURANT
Main entrance on Bridge Street

Overflowing dustbins stood against one wall. "Look at this!" Andi said, darting forward. Food wrappers were strewn on the ground around the bins. "This is just the kind of place Buddy would go digging for something to eat."

A dark-haired man dressed in a white chef's apron and blue checked trousers looked out of the back door. "Hey, what are you kids up to?"

"We're looking for a lost dog," Tristan told him. "Have you seen one?"

"Actually, yeah. There was a dog nosing around here earlier," the chef said.

"A Jack Russell?" Andi burst out.

The chef shrugged. "I don't know much about dogs. A little one – brown-and-white. He was here this morning, maybe about eleven o'clock."

"What happened to him? Where did he go?" Andi demanded breathlessly.

"He looked hungry. I gave him a slice of pizza. Then the boss came and yelled at him. He doesn't like dogs, Mr Vialli. So he ran off."

"Which way did he go?" Tristan asked.

"That way." The chef pointed along the alley.

"Can I give you my phone number?" Andi begged. "In case he comes back?"

" 'Course you can." The chef took a notebook and pen out of the pocket of his apron.

Andi wrote down her number quickly, then she and Tristan hurried along the alley in the direction the chef had pointed. There was no trail to follow now – Buddy's muddy paws must have dried while he was behind the restaurant – but Andi was sure he was nearby. Her heart turned somersaults at the thought of picking him up and giving him a big hug. "Buddy!" she yelled as they ran. "Buddy, where are you, boy?"

But there wasn't any bark in reply, and soon Andi and Tristan reached a busy street, lined with shops and houses with front doors that opened straight on to the pavement. Andi's spirits sank – there were no hiding places here for a small dog.

"Where to now?" Tristan asked, raising his voice to make it heard above the rumble of a passing van.

"I don't know, *everywhere!*"

They searched for ages, going into every shop and even knocking on a few front doors to ask if anyone had seen Buddy. Every time the answer was the same – nobody had seen a lost dog.

"We'd better go," Tristan said after they'd been searching for half an hour or more. "Your mum'll be worried."

"OK." Andi knew it was hopeless. Buddy wouldn't have stayed here with all this traffic speeding past. The roads round their house in Texas had been very quiet, and big lorries always made him nervous. "But we should come back later and put up some posters," she added, "just in case Buddy turns up for another slice of pizza."

Judy Talbot was already at home when Andi and Tristan got there. She'd come straight home from work so she could finish unpacking. There were only two boxes of DVDs in the living room now, and cheerful striped curtains had been hung in the downstairs windows. For the first time, the house looked like a home, Andi thought as she led the way through the front door. But it would never *feel* like a home without Buddy there to greet her when she came in.

"Has anyone called about Buddy?" she asked hopefully as she dumped her rucksack in the hall.

"No, love. Sorry," her mum replied, coming out of the kitchen with a pile of towels.

Andi felt a fresh wave of misery flood over her. All the way back from the playground and Vialli's restaurant, she'd told herself that there would be some news of him when she got home. Now that hope was dashed, too.

Forcing herself to think of something else, she

introduced Tristan to her mum. "Is it okay if Tristan stays for dinner?" she asked.

Andi's mum smiled awkwardly. "Actually, I'd planned to have Saturday night soup and sandwiches today, since I haven't had a chance to unpack the kitchen yet." They usually had a casual supper on Saturdays in front of the television.

"Soup and sandwiches sound cool to me, Mrs Talbot, honestly," Tristan said. "In fact, I'd be happy with any scraps you can spare."

"You sound like Buddy," joked Mrs Talbot, then she stopped herself and her eyes filled with sadness. "Poor Buddy."

Andi agreed. "We thought we'd found him on the way home," she told her mum, "but it turned out to be a completely different dog named Scamp. Then we met someone in a restaurant who saw Buddy and gave him a slice of pizza. But he's not there now. We searched everywhere." Her voice trembled and she stopped talking.

"Oh, Andi." Mrs Talbot set the towels down on a box and gave her a hug.

"I keep thinking that Buddy's found a new home,"

Andi said, swallowing hard. "What if he's forgotten about me?"

"Of course he hasn't forgotten you. Buddy will never forget you. You're his best friend."

Andi hoped her mum was right. Anyway, letting herself get upset again wasn't going to help her find him. "Tristan and I want to make some posters telling people that Buddy's missing. Is the computer set up, Mum?"

"Yes, it is. And that sounds like a great idea! Grab a snack before you start, if you want."

They poured themselves a glass of milk each and took a few biscuits up to the study. The computer had been set up on a desk under the window in the bedroom that Mrs Talbot had decided to use as a home office. It was already switched on.

It felt odd to be working on the computer without Buddy. Whenever Andi had worked in the study in their old home, he had laid down with his head resting on her feet, heaving an occasional contented sigh. Now, even though Tristan was sitting next to her, the new study felt empty.

"I think we should write 'lost' at the top, in huge

red letters," Tristan suggested, "to get everyone's attention right away."

"Good idea." Andi typed it in and adjusted the font size until the word nearly filled the width of the page.

"Then we need a picture of Buddy. Have you got one?"

"Tons." Andi reached for a CD-Rom and inserted it into the drive. A moment later, a picture of Buddy filled the screen. He was lying on Andi's bed, looking up at the camera. The sight of his sweet white face, bright eyes, and pricked-up tan ears – one with a white tip – made Andi swallow hard.

"He looks great," said Tristan. "A really friendly little dog."

"He is." Andi rubbed her nose fiercely – she found that helped her stop wanting to cry. "And look here . . ." She clicked on another image that showed Buddy wearing a clown's hat. "This is Buddy at my ninth birthday party. It was a fancy dress party."

Tristan laughed. "Don't tell me, he did tricks, too."

Andi smiled. "Not exactly – but he did steal my best friend Jess's slice of birthday cake!"

They chose a photo of Buddy sitting on the beach with his head on one side – one that clearly showed the tan patches on his body – and pasted it into the poster. It didn't take long to add a few words about him:

LOST: BUDDY
FRIENDLY JACK RUSSELL TERRIER
LOST FROM ALDCLIFFE
CONTACT ANDI TALBOT WITH
INFORMATION

Andi typed in her phone number.

"I think we should add 'Please check sheds and garages'," said Tristan. "He might have got shut in by accident."

Andi tapped at the keyboard again. "There," she said. She checked the layout, then printed a trial copy. Buddy's sweet face gazed out of the poster at her. "Oh, Buddy," she whispered. "Where are you?"

Tristan patted her arm awkwardly. "We'll find him, you'll see. People round here can't resist a challenge! They'll be emptying out their garages to look for him before you can say Jack Russell!"

71

"How many posters do you think we'll need?" Andi asked.

"One for school and a few for store windows. Could you print twenty? That should be enough."

Andi clicked the print button.

"Let's meet up at half past seven tomorrow morning and start putting them up," said Tristan.

"Okay," Andi agreed. Usually she hated early starts, but she'd do anything to get Buddy back. And thanks to the time difference between America and England, she was waking up at odd times anyway. She stared at the posters spooling out of the printer and crossed her fingers under the desk. If this didn't work, she couldn't think of what else to do. Buddy could be lost forever!

Mrs Talbot drove them to Vialli's restaurant on the way to take Tristan home. While Andi and Tristan got busy tying posters to lampposts, Mrs Talbot took one into the restaurant.

"The owner wasn't too thrilled to put it up," she said as they drove away again. "He doesn't like dogs. But I managed to persuade him in the end."

"I hope it works," Andi said.

"I'm sure it will. You know what Buddy's like with food. He's probably asleep in someone's garden a couple of streets from that restaurant right now, just so he's close enough to pop back when he feels hungry."

Andi laughed in spite of her worries. That sounded exactly like Buddy.

As soon as they got home, Andi went to the study to email Jess. She typed quickly, telling her that Buddy had run off and asking if she had any bright ideas for finding him. As she went downstairs, Andi looked at her watch, trying to calculate when she might get a reply from her best friend.

Her mother was in the kitchen, emptying out a box of pots and pans. She looked tired, but she smiled when she saw Andi.

"Can I leave a bowl of dog food outside the back door," Andi asked, "in case he comes back in the night?"

"No, darling. We'd get every fox in town dropping by for a snack."

Andi sighed. Her mum was right, of course, but she wanted to be doing something – anything – to help Buddy.

Later, just before she went to bed, she checked the computer again. Yes! Jess had emailed back already. She must have logged on as soon as she came home from school.

Dear Andi, Jess began. **I am so, so, so, so sorry to hear about Buddy. I hope he turns up soon! The people in your old house seem really nice, and their son, Zack, invited me to play tennis.**

She went on to tell Andi lots of school gossip and some news about a pool party everyone was going to. Andi felt her shoulders droop as she stared at the screen. It sounded like Jess was hardly missing her at all. If they hadn't moved, Andi would be going to that party, too. And Buddy would be lying under the desk right now with his head on her feet.

Chapter Seven

Tristan was waiting for Andi when she raced down to the corner the next morning. She was a few minutes late; she'd been so worried about Buddy that she'd found it difficult to fall asleep at first, and then she'd slept right through her alarm. "Sorry I'm late," she panted. "Have you been here long?"

"A couple of hours," he joked. "No, I'm not that good in the morning. Have you brought some more posters?"

Andi took them out of her bag and unrolled them, blinking hard when Buddy's sweet face looked up at her.

"Great!" said Tristan. "I thought we could put them on those trees." He pointed along the road. "I brought some string. And we'll ask Rachel to put one in her window."

They tied the posters to the trees, then headed for Rachel's shop.

"Hello there," Rachel said, as they went inside. "Have you found Buddy yet, Andi?"

"No, not yet. I wondered if you could put this up in the window." Andi handed Rachel a poster.

"Of course I will." She looked at Buddy's photo. "He's adorable. No wonder you miss him so much."

Tristan's brother, Dean, appeared in the doorway to the storeroom behind the shop. His waterproof bag was slung over his shoulder. He watched Rachel take the poster over to the window and frowned. "What about people who don't go out much?" he said. "Lots of old people sit by their windows all day. They might not see those posters, but they stand a good chance of seeing Buddy run by."

"But we can't knock on everyone's door," Andi pointed out.

"No, wait!" Tristan said. "We don't need to. We could shrink the poster down on the computer and print flyers small enough to go through people's letterboxes."

"Good idea, Tris," said Dean. "I could deliver them with the papers tomorrow morning if you want. What do you think?"

"That'd be awesome!" Andi agreed. "Though Buddy will probably be home by then," she added confidently. Even so, it wouldn't hurt to have a plan in place, just in case.

"I'd better get going," Dean said. He shot out of the shop and leapt on his bike. Before he pedalled off, he called over his shoulder, "You'd better check that the flyers are okay with Rachel. They're her papers I'm delivering, after all."

"Right!" said Andi, feeling herself turn red as Dean gave her a broad grin before cycling off at top speed.

"We'd better go, too," said Tristan. "It's nearly eight o'clock and I haven't had any breakfast yet."

"See you at school," Andi said when they were outside.

"Right," Tristan agreed. "And don't worry. The posters are bound to work. Buddy will be back in no time."

Andi walked home slowly, looking for Buddy in every garden and under every bush. Talking about the posters and flyers had made her feel really hopeful, but there were so many places for a little dog to hide, would *anyone* be able to find him? Even worse, he might have started trying to find his way back to Texas – he probably didn't understand that his trip in the aeroplane had taken him across the sea.

An old man with snow-white hair and tanned skin was unlocking the peacock letterbox. "Cheer up," he greeted Andi with a smile. "Whatever you're worrying about might never happen."

"It already has," Andi replied miserably. "I've lost my dog, look." She showed him a poster.

"No wonder you look so down in the dumps," he said sympathetically. "I'll keep an eye out for the little fella. And I'll put a poster on my tree for you."

"Thanks." Andi handed him one. "I love your peacock feathers, by the way."

"Painted them myself," the old man said proudly. "I love birds. I hope your Buddy doesn't chase them."

Andi shook her head. "Not very often. And if he does they always fly away before he can catch them."

The man laughed. "Knowing Jack Russell terriers, even a pair of wings wouldn't make him give up! What's your name?"

"Andi."

"Pleased to meet you, Andi. I'm Robert Wheeler. Good luck with the search!"

"Thanks." Andi went on again. Suddenly she heard thudding footsteps behind her and leapt out of the way onto a lawn. A moment later, Mike the postman pounded past.

"Hey," he said, skidding to a halt then jogging back to speak to her. "Have you found your dog yet?"

"Not yet, but I've made some posters."

"I could put some up for you while I'm doing my rounds," suggested Mike.

"Thanks," Andi said. "That would be great." She kept a few posters and handed the rest to Mike.

He put them in his postbag. "Good luck," he called, jogging away.

Andi watched him go. *I will find Buddy*, she thought, with a fresh wave of determination. With so many people in Aldcliffe eager to help, surely he'd turn up soon.

* * *

Andi and Tristan pinned a poster up on the school notice board as soon as they arrived. It was odd to see Buddy's cute face surrounded by posters about after-school clubs and activities. "Let's hope it works," Andi said as the bell rang. People began to crowd inside and she was glad to see that quite a few stopped to read the poster on their way to class. Maybe one of them had seen Buddy already.

The first class that day was art. "We're making an underwater collage," Kelly told her. "Everyone's painting a fantasy fish to add to it. Mr Dixon wants us to make them as detailed as we can."

"With stripes and spots and squiggles and anything else you like," added Chen. He held up his painting to show Andi. It was a black-and-white striped fish with a line of spines standing up on the back of its head. "It's a zebra fish, see?"

Andi went to get a blank sheet of paper, stopping on the way to admire some of the fish that the other students were working on. One was painted in rainbow colours with silver fins; another looked like an underwater pig with gills, a snout and a curly tail. Natalie, the girl who'd said Andi wouldn't know about oceans, had painted an elegant crimson fish and was carefully outlining the scales in gold.

Natalie looked up at Andi. "You've got the wrong paper," she said. "You need white, not cream. The cream paper's for writing."

Andi looked down at the paper in her hands. She hadn't even noticed that it was the wrong colour. She hurried to change it, wondering why Natalie was always so quick to tell her that she'd done something wrong.

Andi went back to her seat and sketched an outline of a plump fish with delicate floaty fins. She curved the body so it looked as though it was swimming round a rock. Then she went to grab paints and a jar of water.

As she made her way back across the classroom, her foot caught in the strap of a school bag hanging from the back of someone's chair. Andi stumbled and the water slopped out of the jar. It splashed across Natalie's painting, making all the colours run together.

"Oh no!" Natalie jumped up. "Look what you've done!"

"I'm sorry," Andi cried, horrified.

"You should be!" One of Natalie's friends jumped to her feet and glared at Andi, her eyes blazing. "Natalie's been working on that picture for ages, and now it's ruined because of you!"

"I'm sorry," Andi said again. "I tripped and . . ." She trailed off, feeling helpless.

Mr Dixon came over. "What's the trouble here? Sit down, Lorna," he said to Natalie's friend. "There's no need to make such a fuss." He looked down at the ruined painting. "Uh-oh." He picked it up, but the water had soaked into the paper and it tore. "I'm afraid this has had it. After all your hard work, too. You'll just have to start again. I'm sorry, Natalie. At least now you'll have some good ideas to get you started again quickly."

Natalie and Lorna glared at Andi. "It was *her* fault," snapped Lorna, jabbing an accusing finger in Andi's direction.

"It was an accident—" Andi began.

"All right, ladies," Mr Dixon cut in, "if you leave bags lying around on the ground, they're going to be tripped over. Now, go and sit down, Andi, and stop worrying. Natalie, get another piece of paper, and make sure that bag is out of the way."

Scarlet with shame, Andi went back to her table. She set to work on her painting, bending low over the paper so she wouldn't have to look at anyone else. Kelly leant across to her. "Don't worry. Natalie Lewis always acts like she's the teacher round here! Everyone knows it was an accident."

Chen looked at Andi's empty jar. "Here," he said, pushing his jar of water towards her, "you can share mine."

"Thanks." Andi smiled at him. She glanced back at Natalie Lewis to see if she was still mad about the fish painting, but Natalie was bending over her painting again and didn't look up.

When the bell rang to end the school day, Andi ran out to meet Tristan. She was desperate to get home and see if anyone had called about Buddy.

Tristan was eager to get to work as well. "Let's go down the high street and put up some posters."

"Right, but we'll have to go back to my house and collect them first," Andi said.

When they got home, Mrs Talbot was at the top of a stepladder in the hallway, hammering in a picture hook. "Hi, you two," she said. "My meetings ended early, so I came straight home. I've finally almost finished with all this moving!"

Andi noticed that the message light was flashing on the phone. "There's a message!" she whooped. Perhaps the posters had worked already!

"Is there?" Her mum stopped hammering and climbed down from the ladder. "I didn't hear the phone ring. It must have been while I was taking empty boxes out to the back garden."

"This could be the next clue about Buddy!" Tristan said, giving Andi a thumbs-up.

Her bad day suddenly forgotten, Andi pressed the play button on the phone.

Chapter Eight

"Hello? Hello?" An old lady's shaky voice crackled out of the phone's voicemail. "Oh, it's a machine. Well, I saw your poster," she continued.

They were right! It *was* a message about Buddy! Andi crossed her fingers for luck, then grinned at Tristan when she saw that he'd done the same.

"I've seen a dog," said the old lady. "It was in my garden, barking at squirrels."

Andi's grin widened. "Buddy barks at squirrels!" she burst out. Her mum nodded and put a finger to her lips, warning Andi to keep listening.

"He was tan-and-white, just like the picture on the poster. He reminded me of a little dog I once had, called Mickey. He used to bark at squirrels, too, and – well, I thought it might be your lost dog," the lady said. There was a click and the message ended.

"Is that all? She didn't leave her phone number!" Andi cried, dismayed. "How can we find her?"

Her mum shook her head sadly. "I'm afraid we can't."

"You could try dialling 1471," Tristan suggested. "That way you'll find out the old lady's number and you can call her back."

"Of course! Tristan, you're brilliant!"

"Shame Miss Ashworthy doesn't think so," Tristan joked.

As Andi reached for the receiver, the phone started to ring. She snatched it up, wondering if it was the old lady ringing back. "Hello," she said eagerly.

"Can I speak to Mark, please?" a man's voice asked.

"I'm sorry, there's nobody here called Mark."

"Sorry, I must have called the wrong number." The man rang off.

Dismayed, Andi replaced the phone. "Wrong number," she groaned. "And now I won't be able to get the old woman's number." She sank down on the bottom stair. "If I dial 1471 now, I'll just get that man's number instead."

Mrs Talbot put her hammer down on top of a box with a sigh. "Well, at least it means people have seen the posters, right? And if one person has seen Buddy, then another person might."

Andi nodded glumly. "I suppose so. But what awful luck! Why did that man have to ring right then?"

"It was bad luck," her mum agreed. "But you'll find Buddy if you keep working at it. Are you going to put up some more posters?"

"Yes."

"At this rate, there won't be a person in Aldcliffe who isn't keeping an eye out for Buddy," her mum reassured her. "Now, I'd better do a bit more unpacking." She disappeared into the kitchen.

"Maybe the old woman will call back," suggested Tristan.

"I bet she won't!" Andi cried despairingly. "This is worse than not hearing anything!" Her eyes filled with tears and she turned away to hide them from Tristan.

"If it *is* Buddy she's seen, at least you know he's OK," Tristan pointed out.

"But we still don't know where he is," Andi replied dismally. She felt sick when she thought of how close they'd come to getting him back. If only the woman had called later in the day, when Andi had been at home. If only her mum hadn't been out in the garden. "I hope that lady leaves some food out for him," she said.

"Even if she doesn't put food out, if she doesn't hear from you, she might call again. But right now, we need to print out those flyers to take over to Rachel's shop," Tristan reminded her.

Andi blew her nose. "OK." She knew Tristan was right. They had to keep working at finding Buddy, but all she wanted to do was curl up on her bed and think about all the things she had done with her dog. "Maybe we should put some extra wording on the posters," she said, "so people know to give their number if they leave a voice message."

"I don't think you need to do that, darling," said Mrs Talbot, appearing at the kitchen door. "Most people will leave their number automatically.

That was really bad luck, what happened with the old lady."

"I suppose so," Andi agreed. Her mum was right; the posters had worked, it was just the worst luck in the world that the only person who had called hadn't let them know how to get in touch with her.

As soon as the flyers were printed, Andi emptied out her rucksack and put them inside, along with the remaining full-size posters. Then she and Tristan set off for Rachel's shop.

Along the road they passed several posters that Mike had stuck up. "There can't be anyone round here who doesn't know your dog's missing," Tristan remarked with satisfaction.

Andi nodded, still upset about the useless phone message.

Rachel was busy stacking boxes of cheesy biscuits onto shelves when they arrived at the shop. "Any news of Buddy?" she asked as soon as they pushed open the door.

"No," Andi replied. "We brought some flyers to go in Dean's newspapers, though, if that's OK with you."

"Of course. If you don't get a few phone calls from those, I'll be astonished."

Andi wished that the shopkeeper's confidence would make her feel better. "Actually, an old lady already called to say she'd seen a dog like Buddy, but she didn't leave her number."

Rachel clicked her tongue sympathetically. "Maybe she'll call back."

"That's what I said," Tristan told her. "Now we've got to finish putting up these posters."

It was only a five-minute walk from Rachel's shop to the high street. As they turned into it, Tristan switched into estate agent mode again. He seemed to be trying really hard to keep Andi cheerful, and she felt a flash of gratitude towards him.

"High Street is considerably older than most of the houses in Aldcliffe," he began, gesturing grandly with his arms. "Built in the early 1890s, it contains a number of buildings of interest. Here we have the Pizza Palace." He pointed to a red-brick building with a pizzeria on the ground floor. " 'Is it any good?' you ask," he continued. "Let me tell you, their pizzas are to die for!"

Andi forced a smile. "Great," she said half-heartedly.

Tristan took her arm and steered her along the high street, past clothes shops, toy shops, shops selling china, bookshops, and sweet shops. They passed a bowling alley and a cinema covered in posters advertising the latest films. Bowling and films were two of Andi's favourite things. She made up her mind to come back here as soon as Buddy was home. She wouldn't be able to enjoy anything until she knew where he was.

The street was scattered with restaurants too – Thai, Indian, a burger bar, – all places where Buddy might have gone looking for a snack, but Tristan propelled Andi past all of them, his eyes fixed on the road ahead.

"Wait, we could be checking out these restaurants!" she protested.

"We can do that on the way back," he said a little breathlessly. "There's something I want you to see." He stopped so suddenly that Andi bumped into him and had to grab her bag to keep it from slipping off her shoulder. "There!" Tristan announced.

They were standing outside the most

extraordinary café Andi had ever seen. The building was painted sunshine-yellow and every table outside had a rainbow-striped umbrella. "This," Tristan announced, leading the way in, "is the Banana Beach Café. And if anything can cheer you up – apart from finding old Bud, of course – it's this place."

To Andi's astonishment, a blue-and-green parrot was strutting along the counter at the far end of the room. "Bananas!" he squawked as they went in. "More bananas!"

Andi burst out laughing. "Wow! Does he always say that?"

"Yes. Jango, the guy who runs this place, truly believes he can serve bananas with *anything*. You don't want to test him out on this. I once had a tuna and banana sandwich and it was *disgusting!*"

Just then, a beaming, round-faced Jamaican woman came out of a doorway draped with strings of multicoloured, rattling beads. She was wearing a dress the colour of sunflowers. "I thought I heard voices! Hey, Jango, come and meet Tristan's young lady."

Andi felt herself blushing. "I'm not—" she began at the same time as Tristan said, "She's not—"

But the woman was still talking. "Sit down, sit down. What do you feel like today? How about banana oatmeal cookies? Or banana brownies?"

"Two Banana Spice smoothies — unless you'd prefer straight apple juice, Andi. They make it from the apples grown round here, and it's the best thing after the smoothies."

"No thanks, a Banana Spice smoothie sounds great."

They sat down under one of the striped umbrellas, which covered the tables inside as well.

Maggie Pearce turned towards the back of the café. "Jango! Where is that husband of mine?"

A man in his mid-fifties with greying hair appeared in the doorway. A plastic apron decorated with palm trees was stretched over his big stomach. "What's all the noise about, Maggie, my sunshine girl?" he asked, laughing. "We got a customer who doesn't like bananas?"

"Bananas!" shrieked the parrot. "More bananas!"

"The parrot's name is Long John Silver," Tristan told Andi.

"He's the laziest parrot in the whole world,"

Maggie added. "Doesn't fly, just walks. Isn't that right, Jango?"

"Sure is. Did you come for another tuna and banana sandwich, Tristan?" teased Jango.

"No, thanks," Tristan replied hurriedly. "I brought my friend, Andi. She just moved here from Texas."

"Texas! I bet Aldcliffe feels a bit cold and grey after that! Well, you've come to the right place if you want sunshine," cried Maggie. "This is the sunniest café in the whole of Lancashire."

"Bananas!" squawked Long John Silver, hopping from foot to foot.

"And the one with the most bananas!" Jango added with a chuckle.

"This is a great place," Andi whispered to Tristan as the Pearces went to prepare their order. "I really like Jango and Maggie. And they're right – it *does* feel sunny. Almost as sunny as Texas."

Andi's Banana Spice smoothie was so thick, she wondered if she should ask for a spoon instead of the rainbow-coloured straw Maggie gave her. "This is amazing," she said, sipping it. There was banana in it, for sure, and spices that she couldn't name, and the sweet tang of apple juice too.

"You should try the brownies sometime," Tristan said. "They're out of this world."

Maggie came bustling over to clear their glasses as soon as they'd finished. "Would you mind putting up a poster for us, Maggie?" Tristan asked.

Andi took one out of her bag and handed it to Mrs Pearce. "You've lost your dog?" Maggie asked, reading it. "That's just terrible. Terrible! And he looks like such a sweetie."

Jango came out of the back room. "Who lost their dog?"

"Andi," Tristan told him.

"Tell you what, Andi," Jango suggested. "I'll call Fisher, our son. He's a vet at the RSPCA centre. Maybe someone's taken your dog there."

"Thanks," Andi said. "That would be really kind of you. My mum called when Buddy first disappeared, but maybe someone's brought him in since then."

They said goodbye to the Pearces and went on along the high street, weaving in and out between shoppers. Tristan stopped outside an estate agents'. The window was full of photos of houses that looked similar to Andi's new house. "This is my mum and dad's office," he explained. Inside, Andi saw a sandy-haired man with almost as many freckles as Tristan sitting behind a desk, talking on the phone. A pretty, dark-haired woman was pulling folders out of a filing cabinet. There were several customers waiting to be served.

"Do you want to go in and say hi?" Andi suggested.

"No, they look pretty busy." Tristan banged on the window. His parents looked up, and he and Andi waved before hurrying on.

"Let's go in here," Tristan said when they were almost at the end of the high street. They'd reached a pet shop with a brightly-coloured sign saying PAWS FOR THOUGHT above the window. A golden cocker spaniel was sitting in the window, watching them with his ears pricked and his tail wagging lazily. Behind him was a huge stack of tinned cat food; Andi wondered how the spaniel had managed to squeeze past without knocking all the tins over.

She followed Tristan inside. The store smelt of dog biscuits and, for a moment, Andi felt comforted by the familiar smell. Then she spotted a special offer on the brand of shampoo that she used for

Buddy and, afraid that she might start crying, she turned her attention to the glass tanks that filled the far wall.

In one, three young gerbils scampered around in the sawdust, playing a chasing game. Above them, a huddle of hamsters dozed contentedly. A pair of fluffy chinchillas were grooming their soft grey fur, and two green snakes stared out of a large tank on the top shelf, their bodies perfectly still but their tongues flicking in and out. A young monitor lizard scurried to the side of yet another tank and gazed at Andi and Tristan, its tail sweeping from side to side.

While Andi looked at the animals, the cocker spaniel jumped down from the window and trotted over. He jumped up and nudged her hand with his nose, eager to be stroked.

"Hi there, boy," Andi said, crouching down to run her hand over his silky fur. His coat was even softer than Buddy's and she felt a twinge of guilt and sadness about making a fuss of him, in case she never got to stroke Buddy's coat again.

"Hello there! I see you've met Max," said a cheery voice. A woman in her late twenties appeared from a back room. She was wearing jeans and a dark-green sweatshirt with the Paws for Thought logo – a dog's paw print surrounded by the store name – printed on the front. Her curly dark hair hung to her shoulders and her green eyes were warm.

"He's very friendly," Andi said, as the cocker spaniel twisted his head round to lick her wrist.

"He probably hopes you've got a treat in your pocket! Max thinks people only exist to spoil him." The woman spotted Tristan, who was standing behind a tall wooden bird feeder. "Oh, hi, Tris. I didn't see you there. What can I do for you?"

"This is Andi," said Tristan. "She's lost her dog. Andi, this is Christine Wilson, my mum's cousin. She owns the shop."

"Lost your dog?" Christine said. "That's terrible! What breed is he?"

"A Jack Russell terrier. Look, we've made some posters," Andi told her, taking them out of her rucksack. "We wondered if you'd put one in your window."

"Of course I will. I'll do it right away." Christine took the poster and headed for the window. Max trotted behind her.

"I can't think of anything worse than losing your dog," Christine said, when she'd stuck the poster to the glass panel on the door. She stroked Max's velvety ears and he sat down contentedly and leant against her leg. "I don't know what I'd do without this old boy to keep me company."

"How old is Max?" Andi asked.

"Ten, and he's just starting to act his age, although he still behaves like a puppy sometimes. He likes nothing better than lying in a patch of sun in the shop window and keeping an eye on things. Oh, and riding in my van! He gets pretty mad if I leave him behind when I go out to make my deliveries!"

As if he'd had enough of being talked about, Max licked Christine's hand then squeezed past the cans of cat food and flopped down in the window again.

"Well, we're off," Tristan said. "We've still got a few posters to put up."

"I'll call if I hear anything," Christine promised.

As Tristan and Andi hurried out of the shop, Andi's mobile phone rang. She pulled it out and pressed a button. "Hi, Mum," she said.

"Where are you?" her mother asked.

"Outside the pet shop in the high street."

"Stay right where you are. I'm coming to pick you up."

"Why? What's happened?" Andi cried, but her mum had already hung up.

"What was *that* all about?" Tristan asked.

Andi shrugged. "I'm not sure, but my mum's coming to pick us up. She wants us to wait here." She gazed along the road, hopping from foot to foot with impatience. Had somebody called with news of Buddy? Was her mum going to take them to him? Or was it bad news? Maybe that was why she hadn't explained.

It seemed like ages before Mrs Talbot drew up beside them in her car.

"Jump in!" she cried, throwing open the door. "I just got a call from someone who's found a stray dog!"

Chapter Nine

Andi could hardly breathe as they drove across town. Any moment now she would be hugging Buddy again! She glanced at Tristan and saw that he looked as pleased as she did, even though he'd never actually met Buddy.

Mrs Talbot pulled the car over to the kerb.

"Is this the place?" Andi asked.

"No, I just need to look at the map," she replied.

"What's the address?" Tristan asked. "I might know the way."

"Cardington Avenue."

"Turn right at the end of this road, then it's the second on the left."

"Thanks." Mrs Talbot pulled away again. "We're lucky to have you with us, Tristan."

"You can tell my parents are estate agents," he laughed.

Andi stared impatiently out of the window. She knew her mum was driving as fast as she reasonably could, but it still felt too slow. At last they parked in front of a red-brick house with a tiny front garden dotted with discarded toys. Andi scrambled out of the car and raced up the path to ring the doorbell. Tristan and her mum were close behind her.

The door opened and a man with brown hair and glasses opened the door. "We've come about the dog you found," Andi explained in a rush.

The man looked very relieved to see them. "I'm Mr Campbell. Come in." He stood back and they stepped into the hallway. "We found him on our doorstep when we came home from shopping about half an hour ago."

Andi gazed round eagerly, expecting to see Buddy charging towards her when he heard her voice.

"He's through here, playing with my daughters," Mr Campbell explained. "Emma, who's four, wanted to keep him, but Sara, her older sister, saw your phone number on a poster and insisted that I call you immediately." He opened a door and ushered them into a sunny room with huge windows. "Hey, girls! Looks like we've found Blackie's owner!"

Andi heard Tristan echo, "Blackie?" behind her, sounding rather puzzled.

Two little girls in dungarees, with matching blonde pigtails, were kneeling on the floor with a dog. It wriggled away from them and bounded towards Andi, wagging its tail.

"Is this the dog you found?" Andi said in dismay. This wasn't Buddy. It was a handsome black Labrador.

Andi blinked hard. How could they have thought that this was her dog? He didn't look anything like the picture on the poster!

The Labrador licked her hand, then jumped round her, his tongue lolling in a huge doggy grin. His coat was thick and shiny, and his eyes were bright. He was obviously very well cared for. Somewhere, his owners must be going frantic with worry, just like Andi was over Buddy.

"I found your poster," said the older girl proudly. "I brought the piece of paper home so Daddy could call you about Blackie." She showed Andi an untidy scrap of paper. It wasn't the whole poster, just the part with the phone number. Buddy's photo and his description had been torn off.

"Is there something wrong?" asked Mr Campbell, obviously wondering why Andi didn't seem happier to see the dog.

"I'm afraid this isn't Buddy," Mrs Talbot explained, putting her arm round Andi's shoulders.

"Oh, no! I'm so sorry," said Mr Campbell. "It didn't occur to me that there might be *two* missing dogs. When Sara told me about your poster I assumed . . ." He tailed off. "You must be so disappointed."

"Let's go home, Mum," said Andi, turning away. "We've got to keep searching for Buddy. Someone might have called while we were out."

"Yes, yes, of course," said Mr Campbell. He shifted uncomfortably from one foot to the other. "I'm not sure what to do now," he admitted. "I mean, what's the best thing to do if you find a lost dog? He's a lovely dog, young Blackie – at least, that's what my girls call him – but we can't keep him here. This house is much too small, and my wife and I work all day."

Tristan moved close to Andi. "We ought to help find the dog's owner," he whispered. "His real owner is probably missing him just as much as you're missing Buddy."

Andi shrugged. She didn't see how they could help. "Finding a lost owner is probably just as hard as finding a lost dog," she joked feebly.

"Not if he's been microchipped," Tristan reminded her. "You told me all about that, remember? We should take him to the vet so he can be scanned. If he *has* had a microchip implanted, the vet will be able to find out where he lives."

"I didn't think of that," Andi said. She'd been so upset about the dog not being Buddy that she could hardly think straight.

"That's a good idea," said Mrs Talbot. "Tristan's right, Andi. This dog needs our help."

Andi thought about Buddy. If someone found him, she'd want them to do everything they could to discover where he came from. This was the same thing in reverse. She couldn't refuse to help this lost dog. "Do you know any vets in Aldcliffe?" she asked.

Tristan nodded. "Mr Harvey. We used to take Lucy to him. His clinic is on East Road."

"Let's take this dog there then," Mrs Talbot said, smiling down at the Labrador.

"That's very kind of you," said Mr Campbell.

Emma threw her arms round the Labrador. "Bye, Blackie," she said sadly. "I'll miss you."

"Me too," Sara agreed, stroking the big dog's head.

"He's a great dog," Mr Campbell said, "and so good with kids. Let him go now, girls. He's got to go home."

Mrs Talbot drove to the vet's clinic with Tristan sitting in the front seat giving directions. Andi sat in the back with Blackie beside her, breathing in the familiar doggy smell and feeling comforted by the thump of his heavy tail against her leg.

Tristan explained why they were there to the receptionist, then he and Andi took Blackie into the consulting room while Andi's mum stayed in the waiting room.

"Hello, Tristan," said Mr Harvey, looking over his glasses at them. He was a tall man with thinning grey hair and kind eyes. "Have you found your beautiful cat yet?"

"Not yet," Tristan told him. "But we've found a lost dog. We wondered if he was tagged." He introduced Andi, and Mr Harvey shook hands with her.

"I've lost my own dog," Andi told him as he lifted Blackie onto his table. "A tan-and-white Jack Russell terrier. Have you heard about anyone who's found a stray dog?"

Mr Harvey frowned. "No, but if you'd like to make a poster about him, I'd be happy to put it up for you."

"I've got one here," Andi said, pulling it out of her bag.

"Excellent." Mr Harvey looked approvingly at the poster. "I'll get the receptionist to put it up as soon as I've seen to this chap." He laid the poster on top of a medicine cabinet and ran a scanner over the dog. A green light glowed on the handheld receiver. Mr Harvey beamed at them. "Bingo! It looks like this gorgeous fellow has a chip!"

Tristan flashed a triumphant grin at Andi.

"I'll just make a quick phone call to the

microchip registration company," Mr Harvey said. He lifted the Labrador down, then went into the office behind his consulting room.

"Do you hear that, boy?" Andi said, ruffling the dog's ears. "You're going home!"

The dog gave an excited bark and his tail began to wag. Andi grinned at Tristan. "I'm really glad we brought him here."

"Me too. Those microchips are amazing." He fell silent and Andi guessed he was wishing again that his cat had been chipped.

The office door opened and Mr Harvey reappeared. "Well, I can tell you that he's called Jet and he lives with Mr and Mrs Peterson at 31 Holly Drive."

"If his name's Jet, Emma and Sara made a good guess when they called him Blackie," Andi pointed out.

"Holly Drive's not far from where we live," Tristan told her. "In fact, it's about halfway between my house and yours, Andi." He thanked Mr Harvey, who wished them luck finding Buddy, and they left.

"That's terrific news!" said Mrs Talbot when they

told her everything they'd found out about Jet. "Let's take him straight home. His owners will be overjoyed to get him back."

They hurried out to the car and Jet sprang into the back seat as soon as Andi opened the door. She climbed in after him and put her face close to his soft ear as her mum started the engine. "You're going home, Jet," she whispered.

The big dog seemed to understand. He flopped down beside her and rested his head contentedly on her leg with his eyes half closed. Andi's heart lurched. Jet was luckier than Buddy. *Where are you, Buddy?* she thought despairingly, burying her fingers in Jet's glossy black fur.

Jet stood up on the seat and began to bark excitedly when the car drew up outside his house in Holly Drive. He knew exactly where he was! "Shh, boy," Andi said, hanging on to his collar. "You'll be home in a minute."

Jet jumped out as soon as the car door opened, and Andi scrambled out after him and held his collar as they headed for the front door.

Tristan rang the bell. "Jet belongs to Mr and Mrs Peterson, right?" he whispered to Andi, and she nodded encouragingly. A moment later, the door opened, and there stood Natalie Lewis.

Chapter Ten

Natalie frowned when she saw Tristan and Andi. Then she looked down and her face lit up. "Jet!" she exclaimed, holding out her arms.

The black Labrador sprang away from Andi and launched himself at Natalie. She crouched down and hugged him joyfully. "Where have you been, boy? I was so worried! I thought I was never going to see you again."

Andi stared at Natalie in astonishment. She seemed very different to the way she'd been at school. Then Andi caught Tristan's eye, and they grinned at each other. Even if they hadn't found Buddy, it felt good to have made someone so happy.

"Do you want to come in?" asked Natalie when she straightened up again, her eyes shining. She let go of Jet and he bounded round her happily, his tail slapping her legs.

After the trouble over the fish painting, Andi was a bit surprised that Natalie was being so friendly. But then, it was obvious that she adored Jet, and Andi began to have second thoughts about her classmate. She must be a nice person if she loved her dog as much as Andi loved Buddy.

"This is Natalie Lewis, Mum," Andi said. "She's in my class at school. Natalie, this is my mum, Judy Talbot."

"Hello, Natalie," said Mrs Talbot. "We took Jet to the vet's and Mr Harvey scanned the microchip to tell us where to find you."

"Thank you so much for bringing him back," Natalie said.

"Well, I'd better get home," said Andi's mum. "But you two can stay and walk home from here later, if you want," she said to Andi and Tristan.

Andi felt a bit unsure – after all, she and Natalie hadn't exactly got off to a great start at school, with the spoilt fish painting. But she couldn't tell her mum about that now, and Tristan answered for both of them anyway.

"OK," he said. "I've always wanted to see inside one of these houses." He put on his estate agent's voice again: "Holly Drive is home to some of Aldcliffe's premier addresses." They all laughed.

"I'll see you later then," Mrs Talbot said, heading for the car.

"Thanks again," Natalie called after her. She held the door wide and looked at Tristan and Andi. "Well, are you coming in, or not?"

They followed Natalie and Jet across a wide, high-ceilinged hallway and into a vast kitchen. Beyond it was a sunroom dotted with tall plants and furnished with comfy-looking cane armchairs.

"There's something I don't quite understand," Andi blurted out without thinking. "Mr Harvey told us that Jet belonged to some people called Peterson, but your last name's Lewis."

"I still have my dad's name," Natalie explained, "but my mum's re-married." She clicked her fingers. "Come on, Jet. Let's give you something to eat. I know you've only been gone for a couple of hours, but I bet you're starving."

She fed Jet, then poured three glasses of orange juice and carried them into the sunroom. They all sat down. "Nice house," Tristan whispered to Andi. "My mum and dad would love to have one like this on their books."

Andi grinned, then took her drink from Natalie. "Thanks."

There was an awkward silence. The sun was beaming in through the roof of the sunroom and Andi began to feel warm. She pulled off her sweatshirt.

"I love your shirt, Andi," Natalie said. "It's much better than that lavender sweatshirt you had over it."

Andi glanced at her in surprise, but Natalie was smiling in such a friendly way that Andi realized she hadn't meant to be nasty. She was obviously one of those people who blurted things out without thinking.

Andi sipped her drink and hunted around for something to say. "How did you lose Jet?" she asked at last.

"It happened after school. I was taking him to the park, but his lead couldn't have been clipped on properly."

"A park?" Andi cut in eagerly. "Is it near here?"

"Yes, Branfield Park. It's huge, perfect for dogs. There's a whole wood in the middle of it. Jet loves being let loose in there."

"I looked everywhere for some open space!" Andi told her. "I was starting to think there was nowhere round here to walk dogs."

"It's a bit hidden," Natalie admitted. "I'll show you how to find it if you want."

A wave of sadness washed over Andi. "There's no point," she sighed. "Not without my dog."

"Don't you have a dog?" Natalie said with a frown.

Tristan explained about Buddy being lost during Andi's first days in Aldcliffe. Right away, Natalie jumped up and came to sit beside her. "You poor thing!" She slipped an arm round Andi's shoulders. "I'd die if I ever lost Jet for good." Almost as though he could understand what she was saying, Jet came trotting over as well. He sat beside Natalie with his head on her knee and gazed adoringly up at her.

"I'll help you search for Buddy," Natalie went on.

"Really? That would be nice of you," Andi said. She looked from Natalie to Tristan and grinned. "I've only been here a couple of days and I've already made some friends!" She stopped in amazement. Maybe she was beginning to feel at home here after all! If only they could find Buddy . . .

As if he could read her mind, Tristan drained the last of his orange juice and stood up. "Let's get over to the park right now and look for Buddy."

"I'll bring Jet," said Natalie. "Maybe he'll be able to sniff him out." Andi and Tristan glanced at each other in alarm, and Natalie laughed. "Don't worry. I'm not going to let him off his lead this time!"

The entrance to Branfield Park was only a five-minute walk from Natalie's house. "Here it is," she said, turning into a narrow passageway that ran between a dry cleaner's and a Chinese restaurant. "This is the back entrance. The main gate is right over on the other side of the park."

"No wonder I didn't find it," Andi said, looking up at the high walls on either side as they hurried along the path. "I'd never have thought this alley led to a park."

The path ended abruptly, leaving them at the top of a wide sweep of grass that led down to a sparkling lake. On the far side of the lake, the ground sloped up to a wood, where the leaves were already turning red, yellow, and orange.

"Buddy would love it here!" Andi exclaimed. "Maybe he's found his way here already and he's scampering round in the woods right now!"

They passed a group of boys playing Frisbee. Andi stopped to ask if they'd seen a stray Jack Russell terrier, but to her disappointment, they shook their heads.

After circling the lake, they climbed the hill towards the wood. Natalie kept Jet attached to his extendable lead and he darted in front of them, his nose fixed firmly to the ground as he followed one scent after another.

"Here we have a collection of fine homes designed especially for squirrels," said Tristan as they reached the first trees. "The arching branches and multicoloured leaves combine to bring a sense of natural luxury to the area."

Andi and Natalie laughed. Jet pulled his lead out as far as it would go, then looked back hopefully at Natalie. "I'm not letting you loose," she told him. "Not after what happened earlier."

"Buddy!" they called, peering through the trees. "Buddy, where are you?"

A flock of pigeons took off, their wings flapping loudly, and a squirrel appeared on a branch above their heads and stared down at them as though it was wondering why they were making so much noise.

Andi kept her fingers tightly crossed inside the pocket of her jacket. *Please let him be here,* she wished silently.

Suddenly they heard a loud rustling in the bushes ahead.

"Buddy?" Andi cried hopefully.

The bushes swayed and parted, then a brown rough-coated terrier came bounding out. It raced up to Jet and the two dogs leapt round each other, yapping playfully. Andi's heart sank.

A worried-looking woman came hurrying along the path. "Skip!" she called. "Here, boy!"

The terrier pricked up its ears then trotted towards her. "Thank goodness I found him," said the woman as she bent down to clip on the terrier's lead. "I thought he'd got lost down a rabbit hole." She smiled at Jet. "I'm sure you're much too big and sensible to go down those dangerous holes, aren't you?" She clicked her tongue at her dog and went off down the path.

Andi stared after the woman, horrified. She'd imagined all sorts of terrible things that might have happened to Buddy, but she'd never thought of him getting stuck in a rabbit hole.

Natalie saw her shocked expression. "Buddy wouldn't have gone down a rabbit hole," she said.

Andi shook her head. "He might have. He likes squeezing into small places. That's what terriers do."

"I wouldn't want the job of looking down every hole in the park," Tristan said. "There are probably about fifty million rabbits here. It would take a hundred years."

"It's starting to get dark," Natalie pointed out. "They lock the park at night. I'm really sorry, but we'll have to go back now."

Andi called Buddy's name a few more times. Then, reluctantly, she followed Natalie and Tristan down the hill and out of the woods. Her head whirled with pictures of Buddy trapped in a narrow tunnel, deep underground, and she looked down at

the soft, muddy earth. Maybe he was underneath her right now, struggling desperately to escape . . .

Chapter Eleven

"Drama!" announced Mr Dixon the next morning after he'd taken the register.

A cheer went up and everyone started to noisily shift the tables and chairs to the sides of the room.

"Please get into groups of five or six," Mr Dixon called above the din.

Andi looked round uncertainly, wondering if she should go over to the squid-and-jellyfish group. Then she saw Natalie waving to her. "Over here, Andi," she called. "Hurry up. You can be with us, if you promise not to pour water on anyone."

Andi grinned and walked across to her, relieved. Natalie's group gathered round to welcome her. "Natalie told us about how you rescued Jet," said the dark-haired girl, Lorna. "It was really nice of you to take the time to find a lost dog's owner! I hope you find Buddy soon."

"Thanks," Andi replied. Another girl started to admire Andi's rucksack, which was pink and lilac, her favourite colours, and Andi suddenly felt as if her new school was going to be okay after all.

"Listen, everybody!" Mr Dixon looked round at them all. "For this lesson, I want you to imagine that you have just arrived on a strange island. You don't know where you are, and you have to find your own way around. Come on, I want to see you all looking like determined explorers, searching out a new land!"

Andi smiled to herself. She knew exactly how *that* felt!

At the end of the day, Andi and Natalie walked out of school together. Tristan was waiting for them in the playground. "I thought we could try the park again," he said. "We didn't get all the way through the woods yesterday."

"I'll come with you. I know that park like the back of my hand," Natalie offered.

Andi spotted her mum's car parked outside the

school gates. "There's my mum," she said. "What's she doing here?"

They ran to the car. "Get in!" Mrs Talbot cried, opening the back door. "Quick!"

"Where are we going?" asked Andi.

"You'll see," her mum replied mysteriously. Andi could see that her eyes were sparkling. She glanced at Natalie and Tristan who were sitting in the back seat, but they looked as bewildered as she was feeling. Andi knew better than to get her hopes up any more, but she couldn't help hoping this was news about Buddy. She didn't think she could bear being parted from him for much longer.

They turned into the high street and Mrs Talbot parked outside Paws for Thought.

"Why are we stopping here?" Andi asked. For one dreadful moment she wondered if her mum had bought her a new dog to cheer her up. She didn't want a new dog – she wanted Buddy!

Suddenly, she saw a familiar face peering out of the shop window. It wasn't Max, the golden cocker spaniel. This face was white and pointed, with tan-coloured ears like tiny soft kites – one tipped with white.

"Buddy!" Andi cried. She leapt out of the car and dashed inside.

Buddy hurled himself into her arms, all four paws leaving the ground, and she hugged him tightly. "Buddy! Oh, Buddy!" He pressed himself against her and licked her cheek, his body quivering with excitement.

"Wow! So this is Buddy!" Tristan said behind her. "He's as cute as his pictures!"

Andi realized that she and Buddy had an audience. Her mum, Tristan, Natalie and Christine Wilson were standing around, watching with huge grins on their faces.

Buddy squirmed out of Andi's arms and darted to each of them in turn, whirling round their legs until they bent down to ruffle his ears. Then he scampered back to Andi and sat on her feet, as though to promise that he'd never run off again.

"What— Where— When— I mean, how did you find him?" Andi asked Christine in a rush. She crouched down to hug Buddy again, hardly able to believe that he was really back with her once more. "We've been looking everywhere, and he turns up here!"

Andi's mum reached down and touched her shoulder. "Hang on, give Ms Wilson a chance to explain!"

"You can call me Christine. And I didn't find him," she laughed. *"He* found *me!"* She glanced at her watch. "It was only about twenty minutes ago. I heard Max barking – which is very unusual for him – and when I went to investigate, there was Buddy outside the window. I recognized him straight away from his poster. He's quite a superstar round here!" She stroked Buddy's head. "He looked as though he was going to run off when I went outside, but I managed to lure him into the shop with a handful of dog treats."

"That sounds like Buddy!" Andi said, with a grin. She ran her hands along his strong little body. She could only just feel his ribs, which meant he hadn't lost much weight. "He seems pretty healthy, considering he's been gone for so long. Do you think someone's been feeding him?"

"He's probably been scavenging in dustbins," Christine said. "He's a terrier – they're tough and very smart!"

"I still think we should take him to Mr Harvey for a check-up," said Mrs Talbot.

"Good idea," Andi agreed. "And while we're there, can we get his microchip checked? Just to make sure it works in England."

"Definitely," her mum replied.

Andi hugged Buddy for at least the twentieth time. Losing him had been one of the worst moments of her life, but he was back with her now and that was all that mattered. "It's funny to think that all our searching and all of our work didn't help at all," she said.

"Excuse me!" Natalie argued. "You got me as a friend – which might even be more important. And anyhow, how would Christine have known who to call if you hadn't given her a poster?"

"That's right," agreed Mrs Talbot. "And you've learnt your way round Aldcliffe, Andi. You know the town better than I do now! I don't think you'll be getting lost again – which is lucky, or we might have needed to get you microchipped, too!"

"I think we've done an impressive job," Tristan pointed out, "considering we didn't know the first thing about finding lost pets when we started out."

"That's true," Mrs Talbot said, glancing at her watch. "Now, we'd better get going in case the vet's clinic closes."

"Thanks for everything, Christine," Andi said.

"I was glad to help," Christine told her. "Just make sure you come back soon to say hi to Max – and to stock up on Buddy's favourite treats!"

"We will," Andi promised. She stopped just before going out of the door to stroke Max's silky head. "Bye, Max, see you soon," she whispered.

Everything seemed brighter when she went out into the high street. She noticed colourful signs and shop windows crammed with things that might look great in her new bedroom. A bookshop had a display of animal books in its bay window, and there was a fantastic retro striped T-shirt in the window of the clothes shop next door. Shoppers were smiling, and even the sun seemed to be shining more brightly than before.

"You know what?" Andi said, as they headed for the car. "There must be other people in Aldcliffe who've lost pets. Maybe we could help them. After all, you said we learnt a lot while we were looking for Buddy, Tristan."

"We could offer to make posters for them," Natalie suggested enthusiastically.

"Wait a minute," said Andi, stopping dead so that Buddy bumped into her legs and sat down, looking up at her. "I've got an even better idea. What about making a poster to advertise *us?*"

"*Us?*" Natalie echoed. "Uh, newsflash, Andi. *We're* not lost!"

Tristan grinned. "No, I think what Andi means is that we can make a poster to show that we can help other people who've lost pets. Kind of like a special sort of club. Isn't that right, Andi?"

"Yep." Andi nodded eagerly.

Tristan looked thoughtful. "Hmmm, this could be the start of something really big! A pet won't be missing for half an hour before their owner calls us to put us on the case. We'll call ourselves the Lost Pets Club – no, the Missing Pets Club?"

Andi and Natalie glanced at each other and rolled their eyes.

"No, I know!" Tristan declared triumphantly. "The *Pet Finders Club!* And we can ask Christine to put our poster in her shop window and . . . and I could volunteer to help out there, so I can learn stuff about all the different animals. That'd help us find missing pets!" He beamed at them. "This is going to be great!"

"It is!" Natalie agreed.

"The best!" Andi said. She raised her hand to give Tristan a high five, and Natalie joined in.

"Three cheers for the Pet Finders Club!" they shouted together.

Buddy jumped up at them with a happy bark, as if to say that he thought it was a great idea too.

Andi bent down and ruffled his fur. "Do you like the sound of that, Bud?" she said happily. "I thought you might. And you know what? If we're the Pet Finders Club, that makes you and Jet our first found pets!"

book 2

THE PET FINDERS CLUB

Max is Missing!

Do you love animals?

Has your pet ever gone missing?

Well meet Andi, Tristan and Natalie — The Pet Finders Club. Animals don't stay lost for long with them hot on the trail!

Paws for Thought has been robbed! The Pet Finders Club are eager to help find the animals, especially Max, the pet shop owner's cocker spaniel, but there are just so many missing. With barely any clues, this could be their toughest case yet!

book 3

THE PET FINDERS CLUB

Looking for Lola!

Do you love animals?
Has your pet ever gone missing?

Well meet Andi, Tristan and Natalie —
The Pet Finders Club. Animals don't stay
lost for long with them hot on the trail!

A valuable Russian Blue cat has
gone missing, and ... she's pregnant!
The Pet Finders know there is no
time to lose but they've also got their
hands full with a new type of case —
trying to find a lost dog's owner!